His voice was achingly familiar...

Val turned when she heard her name. A thought dashed through her mind, something uncomfortable, as she strove to place the man who'd spoken. Then she recognized him. Quaid Perrault—the ice climber who had fallen from "Death Scream."

Quaid's lips lifted in a brief smile and Val found herself staring, recalling a time when his smile had been very different—easy, almost arrogant—and his laughter had been deep, resonant and self-assured.

But that had been four years ago. She'd covertly watched him then, surrounded by his friends and admirers. He'd been a yuppie from head to foot, self-centered, rich, as egotistical as they came, and she'd disliked him immediately.

Looking at him now, she could hardly believe he was the same man. His black hair was pulled straight back and tied with a leather strip, so unlike the successful businessman's cut he'd sported back then. He was wearing a blue parka and worn jeans. His mountaineering boots were heavy and scuffed.

Still, the clothing, the ominous black patch he wore over one eye, and the scar on his chin were subtle differences compared to his fathomless, haunted gaze.

MEN at WORK

RENEE ROSZEL

VALENTINE'S KNIGHT

MAGNIFICENT
MEN

Harlequin Books

TORONTO • NEW YORK • LONDON
AMSTERDAM • PARIS • SYDNEY • HAMBURG
STOCKHOLM • ATHENS • TOKYO • MILAN
MADRID • WARSAW • BUDAPEST • AUCKLAND

HARLEQUIN BOOKS
225 Duncan Mill Road, Don Mills,
Ontario, Canada M3B 3K9

ISBN 0-373-81061-X

VALENTINE'S KNIGHT

Copyright © 1991 by Renee Roszel Wilson

Printed in U.S.A.

Dear Reader,

I'm excited that *Valentine's Knight* has become a part of Harlequin's MEN AT WORK continuity program. *Valentine's Knight* has always been one of my favorite stories. While researching, I discovered two very interesting facts about men who climb ice. 1) They constitute only 1% of people who climb, and 2) they're referred to as *the hardest of the hard men.* Don't you love that!

I can certainly understand why this intense, rugged breed of men might be called the hardest of the hard—scaling fragile icicles that could snap at any second, carrying a climber plummeting hundreds of feet to the valley floor. It takes an uncommonly brave—and possibly a little crazy—person to regard such a hazardous endeavor as a sport!

My novel *Valentine's Knight* was a finalist for the Romance Writers of America's prestigious RITA Award, and was also chosen one of the top five Harlequin Temptation novels of the year by *Romantic Times Magazine.* I'm naturally proud of the recognition. It's like saying one of my children is especially beautiful and brilliant!

As a writer, I hope you are swept along with Quaid as he travels on his quest to retrieve something elemental lost to him on one fateful, near-deadly climb. And celebrate with him as he learns about love and life along the way.

All my best,

Renée Roszel

To Genell Dellin,
Jean Hager and Lynda Varner
with deep affection

_____Acknowledgment_____

Dr. Andrew Embick is the author of *Blue Ice and Black Gold*, a climber's guide to the frozen waterfalls of Valdez, Alaska—and a driving force among Valdez ice climbers. Dr. Embick not only agreed to answer questions, but gave freely of his time. He even went so far as to read pages of the manuscript!

As well as offering his expertise, Dr. Embick put me in contact with another Valdez resident, Chet Simmons, a helicopter pilot for the Department of Environmental Conservation. Chet made innumerable rescues in Vietnam as an army helicopter pilot and is intimately familiar with this novel's setting. His insight was invaluable in adding scope and drama to the story. To both of these delightful men, I offer my deepest thanks for your kind assistance in introducing the "hardest of the hard men" to romance enthusiasts around the world!

1

> "Build me a son, O Lord, who will be strong enough to know when he is weak, and brave enough to face himself when he is afraid…"
>
> —Douglas MacArthur

THE MAN STARING BACK at Quaid from the rearview mirror was afraid. He had come to know that life wasn't as easy as the old cliché—when you fall off a horse, you simply get back on. At least it wasn't that easy when the fall was from a rotting overhang of ice and the tumble backward was through three hundred feet of death-cold sky.

Though his face was angular and strong, it told a tale of human suffering—the black patch that swathed his right eye, an ever-present testament to tragedy. Sweat beaded his forehead, though the cab of his Jeep was far from overheated in the frigid temperature. His skin, deeply tanned from spending the past two years in the Alaskan wilds, had gone as pale as the surrounding winter landscape as he recalled hurtling earthward, his ice axes, attached to his arms by wrist loops, windmilling about him in lethal circles. It had been a stroke of disastrous misfortune that had caused one of the tempered steel blades to smash into his face.

As Quaid stared unseeing into the rearview mirror of the parked vehicle, his memory flashed him back to endure again the murderous, tearing pain. With a knee-jerk reaction, he cried out, abruptly twisting away, unwilling to witness his own anguish.

With a shudder, he mentally yanked himself out of his lapse into self-pity. The time for regret and self-recrimination was over. He had to get on with his life—get back up on the damned horse and do the thing right this time. There were no accidents in ice climbing, he reminded himself—only acts of incompetence. With unconscious vehemence, he strangled his steering wheel. Incompetence! The brutal word had burned like molten metal in his brain for the past four years, relentlessly eroding his self-worth.

When he climbed out of the 4×4 a spiteful gust of wind welcomed him with the friendliness of an unsheathed knife. Hunkering down into the collar of his parka, he tread carefully on the highway's black glaze. Moments later, when he trudged into Keystone Canyon, ice pellets crunched beneath his boots, the only sound in the vast silence.

He was alone, yet the feeling of being watched crept up his back like a snake. Only a slight turn would put him face-to-face with Death Scream, the frozen waterfall where he'd nearly died.

Having reached a personal crossroads in his life, Quaid knew it was time to begin his emotional healing, yet even in his determination, his body resisted. Licking his lips, he scanned the sky. The sharp, rosy light of sunset was fading, and a flurry of snowflakes pelted his thinned lips, a foreshadowing of ugly weather to come.

More than fifty waterfalls loomed like giant adversaries before him—frozen in mid-cascade. The otherworldly curtains of ice sparkled eerily in the twilight—beautiful yet deadly. Death Scream, the canyon's meanest unconquered route, stood off to his right, aloof and alone, towering one hundred stories above the canyon floor.

Squaring his broad shoulders, Quaid forced himself to turn and confront his fear, yet as he did, he had the uneasy feeling that the world was running at half speed. When Death Scream finally came into view, he could only stare, transfixed, his breathing strained in his struggle to put the hell of the past four years behind him.

After his near fatal fall, he'd spent two years in physical therapy, and it had taken two more years for him to gather his courage to come back to Valdez. Now that he was here, it seemed as though minutes, not years, had gone by, and he wasn't sure he was ready.

He sucked in a breath to calm himself, hardly noticing the burning rush of cold air that stung his lungs. "Stubborn bastard," he muttered, repeating the unflattering tag his doctors had labeled him with during those first bitter months of blindness and pain. He'd become known to the hospital staff, not as Quaid Perrault, but with an almost envious admiration as "that stubborn bastard who should be dead."

It had been a half year into his recovery when the medical center's chief orthopedist had admitted that Quaid's survival had been more than a miracle. His doctors attributed his tenacious clinging to life to an inhuman determination not to give in.

What they hadn't known was that Quaid had lived his entire life that way—first, clawing his way out of a hellish family life to become not only successful, but ruthlessly so. At the time of his fall, Quaid had been a daring corporate raider, a multimillionaire by the time he was thirty-two, simply because he didn't have the temperament that would allow him to lose—at anything. He knew that his survival hadn't been so much a miracle as a genetic predetermination to be bulldog stubborn, and to take "no", not as an answer, but as a challenge.

"I am, you know..." he muttered at the monochromatic emptiness, his jaws tight, "a stubborn bastard." Nostrils flaring his disdain, Quaid suddenly felt stronger for the mere admission. "And you, my friend, are nothing but a chunk of ice.

"You didn't defeat me." His hard-fought confession frosted the night air. "I defeated myself. But—" he whispered a rough vow "—it won't happen again."

He swallowed a deep breath and turned away, hunched down in his parka. Tramping back to his Jeep, he frowned thoughtfully, feeling that at last he'd taken the painful first step of his healing journey.

As he maneuvered the four-wheeler onto the highway, Quaid wondered what his friends in Valdez would say when he showed up for the ice-climbing festival. Would they tell him they admired him for his guts or call him a crazy, one-eyed fool?

His lips twisted ruefully. Did he really give a damn?

VAL DROPPED DOWN heavily onto one of the empty crates that served as furniture in the drafty airport hangar. With the shroud of doom settling onto her slender shoulders, she pulled off her yellow baseball cap and cupped it over the knee of her yellow coveralls. Anxiously she began to tap the red lettering over the bill that read Sourdough WhirlyTours.

"I'm getting feedback in the controls, Slim," she called out, her voice echoing in the cavernous shelter, "and the hydraulic pump's cavitating."

She brushed back her mane of brown-blond hair and laughed without humor. "That Department of Natural Resources guy went white as a sheet when the chopper

started howling like a wounded bear over Valdez glacier. He thought he was going to die right there. When
we landed, he did everything but kiss the ground."

Slim ambled around the lemon-yellow helicopter,
shaking his bald head and wiping his greasy hands on
a rag. His shaggy mustache lifted, so she knew he was
grinning at her remark, but his smile didn't reach his
smoky hazel eyes. It was obvious that he was avoiding
eye contact, and she felt sick. "So," she guessed, "the
pump's shot."

"Like an ol' Western movie villain, Val." He
shrugged his bony shoulders. "Sorry 'bout that. I know
you have a couple more charters scheduled this week."

"Had," she corrected him, looking down at her
hands. "How much?"

"Couple thou. Maybe a rebuilt for about half."

She exhaled slowly and then glanced up, smiling
halfheartedly. "How long for a rebuilt?"

"Too late for your charters. With luck, next week.
Have to order it from Anchorage."

She ran a hand through her hair, unconsciously fluff-
ing the unruly curls. "Okay. I'll call Joe Carter—throw
him a little business. With his new baby, he can use the
money."

"I 'spect." Slim shook his head at her. "Lucky you're
so independently wealthy you don't *need* no charters."

She stood and unzipped the coveralls that covered
her jeans and plaid shirt, stepping out of them. "Yeah,
lucky. Say, Slim, could you take a little of your pay in
meals for a while?"

He grinned down at her. "One of the main reasons I
work for you, Val, is you're the best darned cook in
Valdez."

She gave him a quick hug. "I'll make it up to you."

"Hell, how much money does an old leather-skinned hermit like me need, anyhow?'' When she'd stepped back, he squinted down at her, looking concerned. ''You just hit a little stall, 's all. Things'll get better. Always do.''

''Sure.'' With smiling bravado, she waved the problem off as though she had a thousand dollars nestled away in her furry mukluks. ''You just get Sourdough WhirlyTours back in the air. Meantime, Mazie and I'll take a little unscheduled vacation from the daily grind.''

''My ears are burning,'' a twittery voice called from behind Val. ''What are you two saying about me now?''

''We was tryin' to figure a way to get you and me out on some ice sheet alone—in a cozy igloo. We'd live on love and stewed goat.'' Slim grinned at her and winked. ''You like the idea, you handsome hunk o' woman?''

Mazie gave Slim a coy look. ''I'd go for it, but you'd better ask my old man. He'd probably be willing to talk about it—during football season.'' With Slim's loud guffaw, she slipped out through the door that led to the front office, pulling her sweater closer around her ample bosom. ''It's freezing out here. How can you two stand it?''

''The heater's on the blink again,'' Val explained, hanging her coveralls on a hook and retrieving her fur-lined parka.

''That's no news flash, but if it makes you feel any better, it'll work great in July.'' Mazie shivered then added, ''Speaking of what's new—there's a man in the office. Says Ross Knox sent him over. Something about renting a room at your place, Val, since the Ice Festival's got the hotels booked.''

Val's brow creased in a frown. She'd forgotten she'd

promised Ross she'd help with the overflow the town always suffered when ice climbers from all over the world converged in Valdez to climb Keystone's frozen waterfalls.

With a wan grin, she resigned herself to the fact that she could use the money. Turning back to Slim, she said, "Think he'd be dumb enough to go for a thousand dollars for two weeks of room and board?"

"Feed him before ya bring it up—he'll go for it."

She laughed, grateful for his loyalty. "Just for that, I'll bring you a hot lunch tomorrow—and plan on dinner at my place tomorrow night."

Slim gave her a jaunty salute. "Roger, Val. Salmon steaks?"

"Salmon   steaks   tomorrow,   salmon   croquettes Wednesday, salmon hash Thursday, salmon—"

He took her arm and began to tow her toward the office. "Let's get out of here before you get to the salmon-bone-and-old-sock broth." As they walked, he added, "Heck, feed him while you're wearing that red sweater of yours and ask him for two thousand. That way, he'd be a happy little camper and we could get us a brand new hydraulic pump."

Val eyed him narrowly. "Remind me never to wear that sweater around you again—you lech."

He gave her an injured look. "Hey, everybody needs a hobby."

Mazie propped her hands on her well-padded hips. "You ever tried cold showers?"

His mustache rose wickedly. "You offerin'?"

Mazie rolled her eyes. "I give up. Say, Val, about that early charter in the morning, do you need me to be here at seven, or is eight okay?"

Val sobered, drawn back to the problem at hand. "I'm afraid we'll be out of commission for a week or so.

Hydraulic pump. I feel awful, but I can't afford to keep you in the office.''

Mazie gave Slim a quick, worried look before she turned back to Val, taking her hand. "Don't worry, hon. Murph just splurged and got me a staple gun for our anniversary. I've been wanting a little free time to attach things to other things around the house—you know, staple the kids in their closets, Murph to me…'' She waggled her eyebrows suggestively. "Things like that.''

Val had to smile at the older woman's attempt to lighten her mood. "You're a crazy person, Mazie, but thanks—and call Joe Carter about taking the rest of this week's charters for me. Luckily, I didn't have any planned for next week because of the Ice Festival.''

Mazie led the threesome out of the hangar into the comparative warmth of the drab, cluttered office. The VHF radio was crackling, and control-tower chatter filled the air.

"I'll get right on it, Val.'' Mazie headed for her desk. "Joe and I bowl in the same league tonight. I'll catch him at the alley.''

"Well, night, folks,'' Slim said, grabbing his wool coat from a wooden rack beside the door. With a curious little squint, he gave a nod to the stranger lounging in one of the scarred chairs by the window. The man unfolded his lean frame and stood to his full height, dwarfing the tall mechanic. He asked, "Are you Val Larrabee?''

Val turned when she heard her name and looked across the room. A thought dashed through her mind, something uncomfortable, as she strove to place the man who'd spoken. Then she recognized him. Quaid Perrault—the ice climber who had fallen from Death Scream four years ago.

She remembered the last time she'd seen him—bandaged and near death as she airlifted him from the canyon to Valdez Community Hospital. He'd been out of it, moaning, writhing in his pain, mumbling incoherently. She'd never forget his tremendous, dogged courage. Though bloodied and horribly broken, Quaid Perrault fought with all his waning strength to survive. She'd been glad to hear that he'd recovered, and happy to have had a hand in helping him, though she doubted that he would remember any of it.

Before she could speak, Slim responded to his question by cocking his head in her direction. "That's Val over there." He drew a woolen stocking hat from his pocket and settled it over his ears. "I'm Slim Toonon—mechanic." He offered a smudged hand.

Quaid's lips lifted in a brief, polite smile, and Val found herself staring, recalling a time when his smile had been very different—easy, almost arrogant—and his laughter had been deep, resonant and self-assured. But that had been four years ago. She'd seen him eating dinner in the Valdez Harbor restaurant with some of his climbing buddies just after he'd conquered two virgin routes in the canyon. Both climbs had been difficult, and Quaid had had the honor of naming them. He'd been quite the celebrity about town back then.

Val had dropped by the restaurant to pick up one of their special cream pies for her ailing husband. While she'd waited for her order, she'd covertly watched him with his friends and admirers. For a married man, she'd thought he'd swaggered too much and had been far too friendly with the single women. He'd been a yuppie from head to foot, self-centered, rich, as egotistical as they came, and she'd disliked him immediately.

Looking at him now, she could hardly believe he

was the same man. His black hair was pulled straight back and tied with a leather strip, so unlike the successful businessman's cut he'd sported back then. He was wearing a blue parka, not new, and worn jeans. His mountaineering boots were heavy and scuffed. All in all, his attire was entirely too nondescript for a high roller like the Quaid Perrault she remembered.

Still, the clothing, the ominous black patch and the scar on his chin were subtle differences compared to his fathomless, almost haunted gaze. She felt that Quaid Perrault had undergone vast changes in the four years since she'd seen him struggling for his life. His smile no longer reeked of arrogance, his stance held no swagger. Gone was the teasing glitter in his eyes—eye—she corrected herself, suddenly aware that Slim had gone and that Quaid had trained a curious gaze on her.

"Val Larrabee?" he asked her softly, looking more than a little surprised. "I understand we've met...."

She pulled herself out of her reverie and walked over to him. "It's Valentine. And, yes. We met briefly. I was glad to hear you made it."

He shrugged and allowed his gaze to drift away for a minute, obviously uncomfortable with the subject. "Thanks to you," he added. "Sorry it's taken me so long to say it."

"Forget it. It was my day to be on duty. That's all."

"I understand it wasn't an easy rescue—being a narrow, windy canyon. Not just anybody could have done it."

Now it was her turn to shrug and feel uncomfortable under his intent scrutiny. "Let's just say we were both lucky that day."

"Okay—" he nodded "—but I owe you one."

She laughed nervously. "I'll hold you to that, Mr.

Perrault. You can fix me breakfast one morning." Her innocent remark sounded blatantly promiscuous, and she hastened to correct the impression with, "What I meant was—"

"I know what you meant," he assured her without showing even a whisper of amusement at her expense. "And I plan to do my share of the chores. Breakfast included."

With an inward sigh of relief, she offered him her hand. "That's fine. Welcome back to Valdez. I understand you need a place to stay."

Engulfing her fingers in polite greeting, he said, "Yes. I didn't decide to make the trip until early this morning, and Ross's place is packed cheek to jowl with climbers." His hand was cool, but not as cold as hers. And his palm was callused. Val wondered how a corporate raider's hand had gotten so tough.

"I had no idea you were a woman. Ross simply referred to you as 'Val,'" he was saying. "I knew a Val once—a man. I figured you were an ex-air force pilot. Maybe I'd better—"

"Nonsense, Mr. Perrault," she interrupted him. "We're very informal here, and I have a spare bedroom. You'll be perfectly safe with me."

One corner of his mouth lifted, but she noticed his gaze remained solemn. What a sad man he was.

"I'm Quaid to my landlords," he offered.

"Quaid…" She nodded.

"Well," Mazie called, shrugging on her coat. "Wish me luck tonight." She turned toward Quaid. Her expression became tentative. "Nice to have you back, Mr. Perrault. I didn't recognize you at first. You gonna climb this year?"

He inclined his head in the affirmative, answering Val's unasked question.

Mazie's eyes widened in disbelief. "Oh? Well—then, good luck. I'm Mazie Morton. Bowling is my idea of excitement."

He took her hand, squeezing it gently. "Good luck to you, too."

Her cheeks pinkened, and Val noticed that even as scarred as he was, Quaid still had a mesmerizing effect on women. Mazie directed a smile at both of them before scurrying out into the night. A burst of cold air bullied its way into the building, ruffling Val's hair and showering snowflakes over them.

Quaid turned back toward Val, appearing aloof yet somehow noble. "I had a feeling people were going to look at me as though I were nuts."

Val felt a little uncomfortable. "Some people here think anybody who climbs ice is a lunatic."

"Let alone a fool who took a screamer," he finished flatly.

She glanced away when he used the climbing vernacular for *falling*. "You must have known there'd be people who'd think you're foolish for coming back." Val grimaced. She hadn't meant it to come out that way.

"Is that what you think?"

"No. Not at all." She reached for the light switch and indicated the door. "I understand exactly why you do it. You need to be in control, you love the challenge...." With a small shrug and a smile she added, "And you're a little crazy."

His gaze had become scrutinizing. "You climb? I have some blank spaces in my memory, but I don't think I could have forgotten you."

She hit the light switch, glad that her next remark would reach him in the dark. "I didn't climb then. My husband was ill. After he died three years ago, I took it up."

"Oh," he commented softly. "I'm sorry about your husband."

She couldn't see his expression, and she was grateful he couldn't see hers. "John had an aneurysm. We knew it was only a matter of time." Preceding Quaid out the door, she turned her key in the lock and changed the subject. "Do you have a car?"

"Jeep."

"Good. My car's in the shop." She suddenly realized that with her car *and* the chopper out of commission, she was totally without transportation. She laughed out loud. It was either that or cry. "*Lord*— what a day."

"Not the world's best?"

"You could say that." She saw the Jeep and headed toward it, adding, "Everything'll work itself out."

"Good attitude."

She found herself softening a little in her initial opinion of him; she had to admire his positive thinking. Glancing up at his face, she noticed that snowflakes were catching on his long, dark lashes, and her breath caught. Never in her life had she seen such captivating masculine beauty as that fringe of sparkling lashes framing a shadowed eye. She suddenly wondered if he was aware of how attractive he was, scars and all.

Surprising her, he took her arm, helping her across the glaze of ice. "I hope I won't be putting you out," he remarked quietly.

With his sudden nearness, Val became acutely aware of the considerable strength of his body. She consciously took a step away as she said, "No problem. Billy Bob and I just have one house rule—if you want to sit on the couch, be sure and have a handful of squaw candy on your person."

"Billy Bob?" He cocked a curious frown.

"My Saint Bernard. The sofa's Billy Bob's domain, but if you want to sit there, toss some squaw candy on the floor. Billy Bob loves it, so—"

"I get the idea," Quaid broke in, opening her door for her. "No sofa privileges without squaw candy. There's only one problem—I'm afraid I'm all out of dried salmon."

"Don't worry. I keep tons." As an afterthought she added, "If you need to make any calls, we'll have to go back in the office. My phone's on the blink."

Leaning lazily against the Jeep, he inquired, "Does anything you own work?"

She gave him a sheepish little smirk. "Well, Billy Bob's in heat. Does that count?"

"I presume Billy Bob made the medical journals?"

Val couldn't help but grin at his deadpan wit, and she wondered idly how long it had been since he'd let himself laugh. Hauling herself into the bucket seat, she explained, "Actually, I made a tiny mistake at guessing her sex."

"What would have been a *big* mistake?"

She laughed softly. "Go ahead, be smug, but you won't feel so superior when Billy Bob jumps on your stomach in the middle of the night. She loves to cuddle. Lucky for me, I have a door on my bedroom." As she felt around for her seat belt, she remarked casually, "I gather you don't need to make any calls."

"I may need to call Ross Knox."

She slid him a questioning glance. "Sure. Just let me know when you need to call him."

He made a guttural sound that could have been a grunt or—maybe, just maybe—a chuckle, she couldn't tell which. More to himself than to her, he murmured, "I'll do that."

2

THE SNOW THAT HAD BEEN cavorting around Quaid's Jeep took on a pugnacious attitude as they wound back toward town, the pale jumble of high peaks behind Valdez becoming lost in the dithery white night. Turning off onto snow-cleared gravel, Quaid found himself traveling down a winding strip of road carved between ten-foot drifts and nestled against a steep mountainside.

After a few minutes, Val was motioning toward a quaint log house, its weathered exterior half-buried in snow. A narrow path had been cleared from the leeward side of the house to the front steps, where a single light beckoned a welcome from behind lace curtains.

"How old is this cabin?" Quaid asked as he turned off the engine.

Val smiled. "Don't worry. It has indoor plumbing."

He glanced over at her. "I didn't mean that. It's just that I thought all the Valdez buildings were new since the 1964 earthquake. This place looks a hundred years old."

"Not quite that old, but it's old. By some miracle the quake didn't destroy it. I pretty much gutted the inside and started over when I bought it."

"I'm glad you left the exterior authentic. It's a great looking place."

"Thanks," she said, feeling an unexpected thrill at

his quiet compliment. Opening her door, she added, "Need any help with your things?"

"No. I'm right behind you."

She fished around in her pocket for a set of keys as she clambered down from the seat and hurried through a buffeting curtain of snow to the long porch. By the time Quaid had gathered his duffel out of the back, she had the door unlocked and was being aggressively greeted by a huge, mewling beast that looked more wild than domesticated.

After stomping the snow off his boots, Quaid stepped inside and closed the door at his back.

Taking off her gloves, Val patted Billy Bob, explaining, "Actually, she's only half Saint Bernard. The other half is wolf." Pulling back her hood, she began to unbutton her coat. "Billy Bob's mother was a purebred Saint Bernard. Once her owners realized that a wolf had violated her, they were ready to do away with her pups. Slim found out about it and grabbed up all three of them. Handed both me and Mazie one and told us to shut up and like it." She hung her parka on a coatrack near the door. "And that's how I came to own Billy Bob, my adorable little doggie."

"Your adorable little doggie has a set of jaws that could chew up a compact car," Quaid interjected, hanging his parka beside hers. He moved slowly and carefully, keeping his gaze trained on Billy Bob, whose huge black eyes were evaluating him with the same deadly intent a brown bear directs on a person who blunders too near her cub. "She's protective of you, isn't she," he remarked softly, not wanting to disturb the dog any more than necessary.

"Terribly. I guess that's why I feel safe inviting perfect strangers to bunk with me."

"I can see why you'd feel secure," Quaid proffered. "One word from you and I'd be dog kibble."

She grinned up at him. "Well, let's just say you wouldn't be a pretty sight...." She trailed off, recalling the last time she'd seen him—when he had been a very tragic sight, indeed. His brows had knit, and it was clear to Val that he too was recalling that awful time in his past. "I'm sorry," she muttered. "I didn't mean—"

"Look," he cut her off, his expression set. "We have to get past how I look. Let's just admit Billy Bob can't do me much more harm and let it go."

"Oh, no—you're wrong!" she objected. "Billy Bob could do you a lot more harm."

His gaze lifted from a watchful scrutiny of the dog to meet her eyes. She felt uncomfortable as he scanned her face, his features guarded. Her remark had come out without thought, and she could see by his face that he'd misunderstood her.

"I'll consider myself warned."

Val felt terrible. "I meant that as a compliment, not a threat."

"Sure." He shifted his gaze away, slowly reaching out to pat the hairy wolflike head. When his fingers had barely grazed the dog's fur, Quaid froze, whispering, "That growl didn't come from my stomach."

"Be good, Billy Bob," Val admonished the dog, squatting to eye level. "This man is my guest. Now show him you're his friend."

Billy Bob, her fangs bared, slanted Quaid a jaundiced look, but after more of Val's crooning and coaxing, the mammoth hound approached Quaid, sat down on her great woolly haunches and lifted a boxing-glove-sized paw.

"See there." Val stood, folding her arms before her. "She's trying to make friends with you."

Quaid lifted a leery brow. "You're sure she isn't trying to lure me into a false sense of security before she goes for my jugular?"

Val tilted her chin in a mute dare. "Don't tell me you're chicken."

A dismal emotion flashed across his face but was gone before he kneeled to give the dog his hand. "Okay, Billy Bob. I'm willing to be your friend, now don't disappoint me by chewing off my legs while I'm asleep."

When he'd stood again, Val was taking off her scarf and flannel shirt. Beneath it, she was wearing a cotton-knit turtleneck covered by tiny red strawberries. Shaking her hair loose around her shoulders, she motioned toward the living room. "Make yourself at home. I'm going to get out of these mukluks and into my fuzzies before I start supper." Pointing to a set of stairs that led to a loft, she added, "Your bed's up there. I'm afraid I have some exercise stuff scattered around, but I'll clean it up later."

"No problem." Gathering up his duffel, Quaid headed across the open, airy living room and loped up the steps to deposit his belongings on the bed. Downstairs, he heard a door close and he peered over the railing. Val had gone into a room at the back of the living area, probably her bedroom.

He surveyed the interior. Beneath him, through a wide arch, was the kitchen. He'd only seen a glimpse of it, but what he had seen seemed cozy and warm. There had been a cast-iron wood stove, and the cabinets and floor were of spruce, stained a rich brown. Before him, on the wall opposite the kitchen, hunched an ancient fireplace built of stacked native stone. Above the rough-hewn log that served as the mantel, a number of carved ceremonial masks stared inquiringly at him.

The cabin's ceiling was vaulted and painted white between the beams, and there were two dormer windows coated with snow.

The front wall, as well as the wall that housed the fireplace, were natural wood, while the other two were painted a soft mauve, bordered with stenciling. Both the change in texture and color served to reduce the heaviness of the wood. An engaging touch, Quaid decided—just like the woman—engaging and unexpectedly refreshing.

Valentine Larrabee was full of the zest for life, and her spirit was as rejuvenating as skinny-dipping in a cold stream—something he'd tried for the first time last year. He'd grown addicted to the freedom of swimming naked, reviving himself that way, and he had a feeling that Val Larrabee could be every bit as addictive if a man was privileged enough to take a naked dip.... He raised a rueful brow at the turn of his thoughts.

He'd almost felt like really smiling tonight, something he hardly ever felt like doing. The desire, long buried, was nice to feel again. Under other circumstances he'd have been inclined to get to know Val better—much better—but this trip he needed to focus all his faculties on his business. He'd learned the hard way about divided attentions—emotional baggage—and it had almost lost him his life. He'd have to be a very dense son of a bitch to allow himself to forget that now, of all times.

Pretty, lively lady though Val was, Quaid had pressing problems to deal with in his life, and any lapses into libido would be damned idiotic at this point.

Putting all thoughts of the bright, cheerful woman

from his mind, he forced his attention back to his physical surroundings.

A circular rag rug in soft pastel shades cloaked much of the pickled spruce flooring and served to define the homey conversation area where a timeworn brown sofa squatted tiredly, swathed in a pink-and-mauve afghan; the seat cushions were concealed by Billy Bob's bulky carcass. An old wicker rocker sat beside the cold hearth. Near it was a substantial basket filled with bright yarns and strips of partially completed crocheting. All in all, Quaid thought Val's home was a warm, hospitable place—very like his hostess.

AN HOUR LATER, dinner was over and Quaid was elbow deep in sudsy water. As he scoured a handful of silverware, Val risked, "How's the corporate raider business, these days?"

He didn't glance her way until he had the utensils sparkling and ready to be dried. "I quit the business." Rancor laced his tone as he added, "The pirate look may be appropriate for the job, but I lost interest in that kind of work after my fall." He turned away and fished out a pan.

Val felt uncomfortable about having brought up a subject that was obviously hard for him, and was about to interject a new topic when he added quietly, "For the past two years I've been working for the Alaska Department of Fish and Game, studying brown bear down at Gumford Wildlife Reserve."

She halted in mid-wipe. "You're kidding."

He turned to consider her. "No. Why?"

She began to wipe again, but without much interest. "Well, I guess it's just such a radical life-style change. What does your wife think about it?"

Shifting his gaze away, he began to scrub the pan. "I'm not married."

"Oh...?" Val was at a loss. She was sure he'd been married four years ago. Had she stuck her foot in it again? Biting the inside of her cheek, she decided to keep her mouth shut.

After an awkward moment, he handed her the pan, explaining, "Lylith walked out long before I decided to live in Alaska."

"Surely she didn't leave you during your recovery," Val blurted, her disbelief evident in her tone. Even in her blackest moments of resentment and depression over John, she would never have considered walking out.

"It was before the—before that."

"Oh..." Val set the pan on the counter. "I'm sorry. I didn't mean to pry."

"Forget it. Things turn out for the best. Lylith married another jewelry designer, and I understand they're deliriously happy—to quote a friend."

Val gazed up at his somber profile. Something in her had to ask, "Has it turned out to be the best thing for you?"

When he glanced back down at her, it was with a strangely disturbing candor. "I'm still finding out what's best for me. All I know so far is that I like working with brown bears. There are days when it's more challenging than reading a CEO's mind. And when my bears grow to trust me, the rewards are more satisfying than merely raking in money."

She laughed wryly. "Guess I'll have to trust you on that. The boring business of raking in money has never been one of my big problems."

She put away the last glass and faced him, wishing there was something she could do to make him smile.

She had no idea what that would take, so she merely suggested, "What say we grab some squaw candy and try for the couch?"

Quaid glanced over his shoulder and noticed that Billy Bob was sprawled over the whole length of it, sleeping peacefully. He shook his head. "What if we just take the chairs?"

"Okay. I'll do a little crocheting by firelight, and you can have Big Bertha."

As they crossed the living area, Billy Bob raised her head and revealed a menacing fang.

"Don't fret, sweetheart," Quaid soothed. "We give."

Val grinned at his gentle assurance in the face of her dog's hostility. "Do you talk to your bears like that?"

"If I want to live." He lowered himself into the sagging leather; worn-out springs creaked under the unaccustomed weight. Picking up one of her books, he read the title, surprised by it. "'*Signing Made Easy*'?" He regarded her. "You're learning to sign for the deaf?"

She glanced up from her work. "Uh-huh. I'm dreadful, though."

"Why?"

"Probably because I'm not very coordinated—requires tremendous dexterity."

He laid the book aside. "I didn't mean that. I meant why are you learning to sign?"

"Oh." She looked back down. "Passes the time. Besides, maybe someday I'll be able to communicate with someone who, otherwise, I'd miss out on." She tucked her feet beneath her. "Haven't you ever been frustrated because you couldn't talk to someone and wished you had the ability to?"

With a quick, unhappy smile, he cast his gaze toward the ceiling. "As a matter of fact, yes. In my case, my jaws were wired shut, and I wanted to communicate to everybody to get the hell out of my face."

Val's lips opened in a silent "oh."

When Quaid met her eyes again, his dark gaze was shadowed and unreadable. "Sorry—guess I just don't like hospitals much. I think it's a fine thing you're doing." His voice lost its edge as he added, "Are you going to take part in the festival this year?"

"Uh-huh."

"Want to make some practice climbs with me?"

She was jolted by his invitation. "Really?"

"Why not?"

"Because you're better than I am."

His head moved side to side, negating the idea. "I'm rusty as an old tin can."

The fire crackled merrily, and the wind howled outside, magnifying her silence. The last thing in the world she wanted to be was a burden—even for as short a time as one climb. *Never never never* would she allow herself to become an encumbrance on anyone.

As the snow rat-a-tatted against the windowpanes like a thousand jumpy fingernails, Val made her decision. "If you promise to let me know when I become a hindrance."

"You've got a deal."

She cocked her head toward a bookshelf in the corner. "There are some novels over there, if you'd like to read. Sorry, but the TV's not work—well, you know."

"Why doesn't that surprise me?" Pushing himself up, he added, "Luckily books don't blow circuits."

"Or go into heat," she quipped, giving him an opportunity to laugh.

The only outward evidence that he'd even heard her was a slow pursing of his lips, but Val had a feeling she'd scored a minor victory over his troubled demeanor.

When Quaid had settled back in the big chair and flicked on the lamp to begin a suspense novel, Val observed him from beneath her lashes.

Quaid's features had closed as he became involved in the story he was reading, and Valentine found herself captivated by the sharp planes of light and shadow brought out by the stark lamplight. The curling black lashes of his good eye appeared to rest on the ridge of his cheekbone, but she knew that couldn't be true since he was reading. It was just that they were amazingly long for a man—sinfully so.

His lips were full, but not too full to be altogether masculine, and his chin jutted just enough to exemplify his hard-hitting nature. There was a deep cleft in that chin, its beauty made only more dear because of the scar dissecting it.

His hair, pulled back severely from his face, would have been unattractive framing a less rugged countenance, but on Quaid, the style only served to accentuate the pure maleness of his craggy features. Maturity and hard-bought wisdom were etched into his face, and the effect was devastating.

Without really seeing it, she eyed the flickering fire, thinking about the man with whom she would be sharing her home for the next two weeks. Quaid Perrault was completely transformed from the egotistical yuppie she'd disliked four years ago, and she found herself drawn to him.

Fidgeting in her rocker, she stabbed at her crocheting as she floundered in her attempt to recall the stitch she was supposed to be using. Provoked, she reminded herself that she had no right to be attracted to Quaid Perrault—or to anyone else.

VAL PUSHED THE PILLOW off her face, wondering why she bothered to sleep that way in wintertime Alaska. For the sun to have even a bleak chance of awakening her, she'd have to sleep past nine—something she'd never done in her life. Glancing at the clock radio, she squinted at the luminous aqua numbers: 5:47.

With a sigh, she reached over and turned off the alarm, set to go off at six. She hadn't had much sleep, and she was irked with herself and with her mind's shameless wanderings all night.

She heard Quaid moving around in the adjoining bathroom. Glumly she realized she'd have to lie there in the stillness and try not to listen to the sounds of his morning regime.

Even though her intentions were the very best, she could hardly help it; she heard him shave, shower, the rustle of his toweling as he rubbed his body dry… That's when she dragged the pillow back over her head, hoping it would not only blind her, but deafen her and stuff a cork in her mind's aberrant leanings. Quaid Perrault was her houseguest, a fellow climber, and that was all—all he wanted to be and all she wanted him to be.

Her thoughts hadn't dwelt sexually on a man in years. After John had died, she'd been left with nothing to sustain her but her legacy of guilt and anger, and the harsh truth she'd learned about herself. That knowledge had been enough to keep her thoroughly entrenched in her nunlike life-style for three solitary years.

John had died in her arms, and she'd blamed herself—seen accusation in his eyes when he'd realized he was dying. Later, after the shock had worn off, she'd been left with her fury and her self-reproach. Her fury had stemmed from John's preference for a bleak existence and imminent death over taking a chance with surgery and possibly gaining a full recovery from the aneurysm in his brain; her self-reproach was due to the fact that she'd insisted that he break out of his protective shell and go to dinner on their tenth anniversary. She'd even coaxed him to dance. While on the dance floor, surrounded by their friends, John had collapsed and died. How much more time would he have had if she hadn't insisted that he get out of the house? The guilt ate at her every day of her life.

John had been afraid to take the chance, unwilling to gamble for a long, rich life with her, opting to take obsessive care of himself, to merely exist rather than live. Those last four years they had no life, no passion, and her love had shriveled, mutated into a painful resentment of his defeatist attitude.

She'd come to terms with her shortcomings. She was undeserving of having someone else to lean on. And even if she was deserving, she was afraid if she did lean on anyone he would one day come to resent her as she had grown to resent John. She couldn't stand the idea of becoming a hindrance to anyone, especially to someone she loved passionately. She only hoped that John had never sensed her resentment. If she thought he had...

Clamping her jaws tight, Val rolled to her face, her tears darkening the cool sheets.

Since her husband's death, she'd had men friends, lots of them, but she'd kept her relationships platonic, competitive and always at arm's length emotionally. At first, when she'd seen Quaid again, she thought she'd be able to keep enough of her initial dislike for him intact to protect her from any unwanted feelings of attraction. But he'd proven to be such a genuinely nice man, so in need of human softness, she hadn't been able to call up any legitimate antagonisms to hold against him.

Flipping over restively, she tried to put aside all thoughts of Quaid, concentrating instead on a jacket she was going to crochet. The pattern was to be her own design. She loved to crochet—it was so relaxing. Yes, she'd work out the details of the jacket in her mind.

Evidently Quaid's an early riser, she found herself thinking after only a few minutes of mediocre concentration on her crocheting. With a depressed sigh, she reluctantly permitted her thoughts to roam, wondering if living with his bears had taught Quaid to get up early, or if he'd always been the sort who leaped out of bed and jogged ten miles before breakfast. She'd read somewhere that superachievers thrived on very little sleep and lots of mental and physical stimulation.

She grew despondent at the sudden intrusion of a suggestive image of Quaid's physical stimulation, and with a groan, she twisted around to glower out her window. A snowdrift obstructed her view, and she wondered darkly what superachievers did for exercise when there was seven feet of snow on the ground.

A flash of nudity, rumpled sheets and tangled bodies bolted rudely into her consciousness. Irritably throwing off her covers, she banished the image from her mind. Slipping into her warm fuzzies and tugging on her white terry robe, she yanked the sash tight, warning herself sternly that *that* was enough foolishness for one morning.

She heard Quaid leave the bathroom via the door beneath the staircase. The other bathroom door led into her bedroom. Val decided it would be a very wise idea for her to shower this morning in cold water.

When she'd slipped from the shower ten minutes

later, shivering and feeling back in control, she heard a scuffling sound in the living area and wondered what Quaid could be doing. She'd heard nothing from Billy Bob all morning, no scratching on the door to be let out, no whining for food—and now there was that odd sound she couldn't identify. She wondered if Billy Bob was dragging Quaid's dead body around, or, by some freak chance, had Quaid come out the victor, and was he searching for a likely place to hide the dog's telltale carcass?

A throaty giggle escaped her. She must be punchy from lack of sleep to come up with such a ludicrous idea. Last night both man and dog had gotten along famously. Within thirty minutes from the time Quaid had begun to read, he'd inched his hand over to trail his fingers between Billy Bob's ears, rubbing and massaging. Not long after that, she'd noted with some surprise that Quaid had moved to the couch and Billy Bob's muzzle was snuggled contentedly in his lap.

Val couldn't blame the dog. What woman in her right mind could resist being in *that* position—even a large fickle half-wolf hound. A painful urgency sparked to life within her, and she bullied back the improper emotion. If Quaid had been divorced for four years, he no doubt had plenty of willing women at his beck and call. Though she had to admit the idea of being gentled in a man's arms held a certain appeal after all these celibate years, she knew the cost for such a luxury could be great. She'd learned that it was at the very times when she felt the loneliest, she had to put on the bravest show. She had a feeling that her biggest test yet was just over the horizon.

She pulled on a baggy gray sweatshirt before yanking on her long johns and jeans. With her hair blown dry and pulled back in a ponytail, Val emerged from her room looking scrubbed and boyish, filled with a valiant resolve to resist even the minutest attraction she might feel for Quaid.

Inhaling deeply, she savored the fragrance of bacon, eggs and toast. But she forgot breakfast entirely when her glance met an incongruous addition to the living room—behind her couch, a ten-foot ladder loomed like an isosceles triangle with a pituitary problem.

"What in the world...?" she murmured aloud.

Having heard her door close, Quaid came into view in the kitchen's arched entrance. "Morning," he said, spatula in hand. "Are you about ready to eat?"

He looked good enough to eat, in his close-fitting black turtleneck and snug jeans. A little catch in her chest told her that his potent physique, more noticeable beneath the clingy knit, had a sensual effect on her that she didn't relish. His broad chest seemed to beckon her to touch, to run inquisitive fingers over hard yet resilient contours, then down across a flat belly to...

To what? Dammit, Valentine! What is your problem? Didn't we just have that talk!

Arranging her face to hide her self-disgust, she skirted the ladder and joined him. "Smells good." Her compliment sounded a little forced. "You didn't have to cook."

"Now you tell me," he countered easily, seeming in a better mood this morning. "You didn't mention how you liked my addition to the room."

Glad to have a distraction, she glanced back at the ladder. "Lovely. I knew that space lacked something—but I pictured a planter there. Somehow the concept of decorating with construction equipment eluded me."

She took the spatula from his hand and began to dish

out the scrambled eggs and bacon. "Did you have a good night's sleep?"

"Once Billy Bob decided which side of the bed was hers," he commented dryly, following her to the scarred kitchen table.

"Oh, dear." Val felt terrible, but she couldn't suppress a wry smile. "I'm sorry, Quaid. I'll keep her in my room from now on."

"Don't bother. I'm getting used to sleeping with furry beasts."

"I thought gentlemen didn't kiss and tell," she offered, her voice taking on a mortified tone. What kind of a kinky nut was he?

He slanted her a narrow gaze. "The furry beasts I'm referring to are Ruby and Myra. They're orphaned bear cubs. They've been known to crawl into my tent on occasion."

"Oh." What an utter fool she was. With a sheepish grin, she added, "Those hussies."

She was about to seat herself when she realized he was pulling her chair out for her. "Oh, Quaid, you don't have to do that. While you're here, we're not a man and a woman, we're just buddies—fellow climbers. Okay?" When she looked up at him, her smile had vanished and she was unhappy with the breathless, pleading quality that had invaded her voice. She hoped he couldn't tell that she was working at convincing herself of that more than anything else.

Scanning her serious face, he vacillated for a moment, then, without warning, he graced her with a heart-stopping grin—his first genuine show of amusement. "Okay...buddy."

Something nameless in his dusky gaze gave lie to his words, inviting intimacy, and Val needed to reject it, to turn away, but for some demented reason she couldn't.

He was talking to her in a language so basic it had no patience with idle chatter. His expressive gaze was telling her that he'd stolen a glimpse into her mind and he didn't buy what she'd just said. Even more damaging, he'd sensed that she didn't want it that way.

His insight unsettled her, but she had a feeling that even though he was definitely male, and even though he had a tempting touch of the stalking beast in his nature, Quaid was still gentleman enough to abide by her rules as long as she insisted on them—which, of course, would be for his entire stay.

Releasing her chair, he strolled to the other side of the table and seated himself.

"So," he carefully changed the subject. "Aren't you curious about the ladder?"

Still shaken by the impact of his sexy grin, she busied her trembly fingers by clutching her glass of tomato juice with both hands. This hadn't been that superior smile she remembered from four years ago. This smile had been one of genuine interest—quiet attraction. She'd wanted to get him to smile, but *Lord*, when finally faced with the raging sexuality of it, she was shaken down to the soles of her furry slippers.

After taking a long, stalling sip, she cautiously set the tumbler down. "This really is a wonderful breakfast, Quaid." She couldn't quite meet his gaze and opted to look at his scarred chin—not much less distracting. "And I know why the ladder's in here."

"I should have guessed. You wouldn't have had a ten-foot ladder in your mudroom if you didn't train with it."

She shook her head. "No. Actually I bought it last year when I was repairing my roof. But if you want to use it to train on, feel free. I know ice climbing takes a lot of upper-body strength, and I've heard of climbers building themselves up by climbing the underside of ladders without using their feet. As for myself, I just stick to my weights, push-ups—the usual."

"I'll get you going on the ladder," he volunteered, as though she'd made the request. "You'll be amazed at how much it helps."

She took a tiny bite of bacon and chewed it into oblivion before relenting slightly. "I'll think about it."

"Good girl—" he stopped himself "—er, good—what were you again?"

Avoiding that flash of his grin, she provided a bit huskily, "Buddy."

"Buddy—right, right." He shook his head as though the concept was hard to grasp but he was determined to get it.

She took a sip of her juice without tasting it, her thoughts pivoting on how damnably alluring Quaid was. She only wished he chewed with his mouth opened or picked his teeth with his fork—anything repugnant and unattractive would be easier to contend with than having to sit across a small table from this physically arresting man.

And now, with the added punch of that smile…well, the combination would have been nasty, low and manipulative if he'd had the slightest idea he was doing it. But he didn't; she was almost sure he didn't. Quaid was a lonely, troubled man, and something she'd said had made him smile. She was glad she'd finally done it. The man couldn't help it if he had a smile that could melt icebergs.

3

AT SEVEN-THIRTY breakfast was over, but the world outside would still be dark for over an hour. They couldn't head out toward Keystone Canyon for a practice climb until Jake had been by with his road-clearing equipment. As it was, they were snowed in, and they knew it.

This perturbed Val more than a little. She needed distance from this man, and she needed it soon. She supposed she'd been chaste too long for her own good, but she'd never been the type to find satisfaction in casual sex, though she'd had her share of eager offers. Maybe she should have developed a less restrictive moral philosophy. If she had, this curious itch to know Quaid Perrault as a sexual being might not be pestering her now.

Quaid had disappeared into the mudroom some time ago. He'd let Billy Bob in through the back door and she'd lumbered happily into the kitchen, her fur dusted heavily with snow. But Quaid hadn't followed her. As Val had toweled her dog dry and gone through their morning's rite of play, Quaid had remained out back, and she'd begun to wonder about his long absence. His parka was still hanging in the entry, so he couldn't have gone farther than the mudroom—not in this weather.

Just as she'd been about to go check on him, Quaid

reentered the kitchen, wiping his hands on a dish towel.

"What have you been doing out there?" she asked as Billy Bob scampered over to join him.

"Tinkering with your washing machine. Looks like you need a new timer mechanism. If we could get hold of one I could install it for you."

"You could?" She leaned on the counter's smoke-colored tiles. "Well, I'll certainly ask Benny over at the hardware store. Where did you learn about washers—at Harvard?"

"Actually I went to Northwestern." He joined her at the sink, turning on the water and scrubbing his hands. "But I learned about washing machines when I was a kid. A nice old guy let me hang around his fix-it shop after school for a couple of years. Taught me a lot about appliances before my father moved us away."

Quaid wasn't looking at her, and there was nothing to betray any hard feeling about his father or his history, but she sensed that he was recalling a part of his life he'd rather not discuss. Though she was curious about his childhood, she decided not to pry, remarking instead, "I'd be eternally grateful if you could get it working. It's a real pain to have to drive in to the Laundromat in the dead of winter." Quirking a teasing grin, she added, "Aren't you going to offer to fix my dryer, too?"

He glanced her way, his scarred, tanned features easing with a flash of white teeth. "I have it on tomorrow's schedule. Right now, I thought we ought to get to training on the ladder. Sun'll be up in an hour, and we'll want to be heading to the canyon."

She hoped her expression didn't reflect her sudden misgivings. She moved her shoulders in an offhand gesture, "I think I'll stick to push-ups, if you—"

"Chicken?' he chided mildly.

She bristled without knowing exactly why, except perhaps that she might be a lot of unflattering things, but she was no coward. "Dares are childish, Mr. Perrault," she rejoined a bit thickly. "I'm disappointed to see that you'd stoop to such a juvenile ploy."

He lifted a broad shoulder and then let it drop elegantly. The play of muscles under the knit material made a bewitching yet galling display. She veered away to stare blankly at the refrigerator as he responded, "I have no intention of being underhanded or manipulative with you—just annoying enough to get you to try it." He probed, "Why climb ice at all if you don't strive to be the best you can be?"

She had trouble coming up with a snappy retort. He had a point. Pink cheeked, she lowered her eyes only to lift them again in his direction. "Lead me to the damned ladder," she said with a resigned sigh.

"Good gir—buddy." He led the way into the living area.

Billy Bob's claws tapped across the wooden floor in Quaid's wake and then grew muffled on the rug as Val lagged behind them both. Billy Bob scrambled onto the couch for her morning nap as Quaid stripped off his shirt.

Val swallowed. She didn't need this. "You don't expect me to take off my shirt, do you?"

"It's a habit, not a requirement." With his broad, contoured back to her, he reached above his head and grabbed one of the ladder's rungs, hauling himself off the ground.

She studied his tense shoulders and the way the muscles of his back bulged, emphasizing the valley that harbored his long, straight spine. She'd never seen such lanky power before except in magazine ads for exercise equipment, and it had never occurred to her that ordinary men could look this flawless. As her lips dipped in a frown, he grabbed the next rung and slowly pulled himself upward. "See," he said, startling her back to the lesson she was supposed to be absorbing. "Slowly and easily, up one side and then with a body shift, down the other."

After he'd made the entire circuit and dropped down, he draped his arms across his chest and leaned on the back of the couch, assuming a nonchalant stance. "Your turn."

He was entirely too near her. With a graceless shuffle, she scurried under the ladder. Just as she was about to reach up, she turned to look back at him. "Isn't there some rule about it being unlucky to walk under a ladder?"

"You're not walking, you're climbing," he told her patiently. "Quit stalling."

"If you bully your bears this way, I don't blame them for coming after you with blood in their eye," she muttered, taking hold and hauling herself up.

"That's right," he coached. "Slowly...slowly. Now when you feel like you've got a good grip, let go with one hand and move on up."

"Easy for you to say," she gritted between clamped jaws. "This is hell."

"It's worse than hell after a couple of hours and a hundred feet up. You'd rather fall here, wouldn't you?"

"I'd have a rope up there," she announced. "What do I have here?"

"You have me," he told her, and though she didn't voice the fact, his soft promise left her far from composed.

"That's right. You're doing fine."

She'd climbed up one side and was shifting her left arm to the other set of the steps when she looked down, amazed to see how far below her he was. As she was about to mention that, she misjudged her objective and flailed out, causing her body to career crookedly around. With a high-pitched cry, she kicked out in a last-ditch attempt to gain solid footing. The wild arcing of her feet took the final toll of her deteriorating grip, and she let go.

Before she realized she was actually falling, she heard Quaid's sharp exhale as he caught her, halting her ungainly descent.

"Oooof!" was her shocked response as she grabbed his neck and found herself face-to-face—almost lip to lip with him.

His bare skin was warm, the curling mat of his chest hair tangible evidence that her sweatshirt had been shoved upward in her landing. Her flimsy bra was all that separated their flesh—and not very successfully, she noticed, wriggling to allow her shirt to fall into place. "I slipped...." she muttered inanely, noting unhappily that their unplanned intimacy had caused her voice to become an unattractive squeak.

"Oh?" he queried, his lips quirking cynically. "I thought you dropped in for a drink."

He leaned back against the edge of the couch, permitting his gaze to roam over her. "You okay?"

She grimaced. "I feel stupid, but I'm fine. You?"

"Other than the fact that I've got a dog's fangs threatening my butt, everything's intact." He cocked his head back. "Mind telling your bodyguard that I'm not trying to rape you?"

Val was momentarily mesmerized by her closeness to his lips. Watching them lift in an appealing smile was a disquieting experience, and it was a minute before she gathered her wits to glance down over his shoulder. Billy Bob was sitting erect and alert, her fangs bared, her menacing growl making a very distinct point.

Finding her voice, Val crooned in a hushed whisper. "It's okay, honey. It's okay." Patting Billy Bob, she told her to lie back down. "Stay—that's a good girl."

"She convinced?" Quaid asked, remaining prudently still.

"She's lying down. I think so."

Val shifted so that she could see his face. "You can put me down now."

He moved to do so, but when he did, Billy Bob scrambled back up and barked angrily.

"What's plan B?" he asked in a whisper.

She was muddled and strangely disoriented. "You've got me. I don't know what she thinks you're doing."

"Hasn't this sort of thing come up before—I mean when some guy's put his arms around you?"

"That's none of your business."

"The future of my butt is my business. I was just wondering what usually happens to men who—" his pause was ripe with meaning "—visit you? Are they buried out back?"

Her cheeks grew hot with mortification. What was she going to tell him. She opted for nothing, suggesting instead, "Maybe if you walk very slowly to my bedroom door, we could get inside and—"

"I get the idea." He took a small step away from the couch. Billy Bob growled, but sounded as though she were merely warning Quaid that the situation was being monitored.

"And I thought we were getting along so well," he

murmured near Val's ear as he slid another negligible step away from Billy Bob's bared fangs.

"From now on I'll put her in my bedroom when we train on the ladder," she assured under her breath, shunning the urge to inhale his cologne. Reminiscent of a cedar wood on a cool moonlit night, his aroma was intoxicatingly male. It drew her almost as strongly as the man who wore it.

Wrapped so securely within his arms, she was suddenly struck with the abhorrent thought that Quaid must know only too well that, even scarred as he was, he was stimulating beyond a woman's normal defenses. She became unswervingly convinced that he'd taken off his shirt as an added temptation, tipping the sensual balance in his favor.

As he moved nearer and nearer to her bedroom door, she scanned his angular face minutely. What tawdry thoughts were running through his mind? His face, etched with the effort of carrying her and moving without seeming to move, showed no signs of nefarious intentions. She cast a glance toward the bedroom door, and she wondered just what Mr. Perrault had in mind once they were secured behind it? Did he plan to pitch her onto the bed, follow her down and make torrid love to her?

As her alarm grew and churned, Quaid continued to slide his boots soundlessly across the floor. The click of the door at his back was Val's first clue that the mission had been accomplished, and she stiffened, frightened by what she knew to be coming.

Instead of throwing her to the bed, Quaid leaned tiredly against the closed door and let out a slow breath. "Val, the next time you consider getting a pet, think about goldfish."

His strained request took her so off guard, she could

only stare. And then, feeling utterly silly, she burst out laughing. Quaid had not been conniving and scheming about seducing her; he'd actually been scared. Her laughter rose, and she knew she was overreacting by the way he was scrutinizing her, but she couldn't help it. She'd been giving him all sorts of ulterior motives and conjuring up evil intentions, all because of her own overactive imaginings.

So she was a little stimulated by this man. *So what!* Quaid had had no thought of making love to her, he had merely been intent on saving his backside.

Peering at her worriedly, he asked, "Are you all right?"

She shook her head. "Don't mind me...." Searching for any logical answer, she improvised. "When I'm stressed out, I have a tendency to laugh."

A lazy grin slow-danced across his lips. "You must be a riot during an IRS audit."

That crazy, wonderful smile he flashed so rarely was infectious, and she grinned right back at him. How could she have been so dumb, so mistrusting? *Darn it!* She liked Quaid Perrault, she liked him very, very much. With a relaxed sigh, she said, "You might as well put me down now."

"I know," he murmured, his voice growing husky, but not from exertion. "If you don't mind, I'd rather hold you—now that I can concentrate on how pleasant it is."

A warning light went off in Val's brain, but that didn't stop the slow trickle of desire that warmed her belly. She swallowed. Part of her wanted to melt into his embrace and take everything his expressive gaze was offering, while the rest of her was in dire need of leaping away. She found herself too torn to move, so she waited helplessly to see which impulse won out.

After only a few seconds, and with evident regret, he lowered her to her feet.

Astonished by his abrupt turnabout, she murmured unsteadily, "Why did you do that…?"

"Your face went pale, Val." His lips twisted in a bleak smile. Averting the wreckage of his features, he ground out, "Sometimes I forget the way I… Forgive me. I don't know what came over me." Without another word, he wheeled away, leaving her standing alone in her bedroom.

IT WAS JUST THAT RIDICULOUS out-of-place laughter that had made him say it. He'd felt it, and like a jackass, he'd said it. He hardly knew the woman, he had a face like something out of a horror movie, but he'd insisted on making his stupid admission. It was true that since he'd left the cutthroat world of corporate takeovers, he'd been trying to live a life that was more forthright and sincere, but his timing—as far as being attracted to a woman was concerned—was lousy.

With a testy yank, he pulled his plastic climber's boots and his ice tools from his duffel bag. *What an idiot move*, he berated himself. She'd probably ask him to leave, and he wouldn't blame her.

Maybe it had been too long since he'd known joy in his life, and Val seemed to radiate with it. He'd never run across anyone whose presence seemed to change the whole atmosphere of a place, but he'd felt it when she'd walked into the dingy hangar office. He'd sensed even then that there was something special and valuable about her. His body had responded immediately—not in a lustful, animal way, but more subtly, as though he'd found something he'd thought irretrievably lost.

Val certainly represented something he'd lost—exuberance for life. Somehow, back there with her in his arms, he'd felt as though he just might be able to get it back.

But now that he was alone in the loft, he'd regained his perspective. He could gain nothing in his life, not joy, not peace—*nothing*—until he'd proven himself and regained his self-respect by climbing Death Scream.

With a crude expletive, he bundled up his climbing equipment. It was time to get on with the job at hand— to forget the woman and put the stupidity of this morning behind him.

The first light of dawn was stealing in through the narrow strip of windowpanes still free of snowdrifts. Quaid gathered up his gear and was walking, unhurried, down the steps when Val appeared in her bedroom door. They looked at each other uncertainly.

"Ready?" Quaid asked, his voice stretched taut.

She nodded, saying nothing, but when they'd reached the front door, she turned to him with eyes that had grown wide and apprehensive. "Quaid," she began, then cleared her throat to steady her voice. "This morning I—I would have gone to bed with you if you'd asked. There's nothing ugly or unattractive about you. I want you to know that."

Her mouth worked for a moment before she cut her gaze from his. "I haven't been to bed with a man in a long time, and I suppose it was unrealistic of me to think I would never meet someone who made me want to. And…well, now that you know, let's be very careful not to let it happen. I'm asking for your help because I sense that you could use a real relationship…but, I can't. Maybe someday I can have sex without giving a damn, but not yet."

She hastened out the front door, leaving Quaid feeling as though he'd been clouted in the head with a two-by-four. He stared after her as she waded through thigh-deep snow toward his Jeep. In his life he'd been beaten by a brutalizing father, half blinded by an ice ax and mauled by a thousand pounds of brown bear, but in all his memory he'd never been so profoundly affected as he had been by her melancholy confession.

What she'd said had taken guts, and he respected her for her principles. He didn't know her reasons for wanting to live her life in such a sterile way, but he certainly had good reasons of his own to want to abide by her wishes. Still, if he'd been forced to admit the truth, Quaid felt a stabbing regret that he hadn't gone with his feelings this morning and made love to her.

Maybe he'd stopped himself partly because of the other thing she'd said. Deep down, he knew that once he'd known her totally, he would want a relationship. He couldn't imagine how any man could walk away from such a spirited woman once he'd made love to her. But since Val was set against intimacy and he was in no shape to handle it right now, the point was moot.

He shivered more from reaction than cold, but he shrugged into his parka anyway. At least it was something to do.

A snowplow had just cut a circular swath in front of the cabin and was heading away down the road. The driver waved broadly at Val, and she returned a gay wave. She appeared to be at ease, but Quaid knew for a fact that she wasn't. And that made him wonder if she might be a better actress than he'd given her credit for.

Whatever her hidden sorrows might be, Quaid decided he wouldn't add to them. He was in Valdez to climb Death Scream, and he had to do it unencumbered by personal entanglements. If Val had thought she was being kind by telling him she was attracted to him—then, it was the cruelest damned kindness he'd ever had to endure.

4

JABBERWOCKY'S FROZEN SUMMIT loomed another fifty feet above Quaid and Val as they took a breather on a snow-covered ledge that jutted out like a petulant tongue. Val slumped against the frosty rock and massaged her wrists, sore where the wrist loops had rubbed the skin through her leather gloves.

"Tired?" Quaid asked as he settled down beside her and offered her a sip from his water bottle. The question seemed startlingly loud in the boundless quiet of Keystone Canyon, especially since she hadn't expected him to inquire after her state of well-being. He'd said practically nothing since they'd left the cabin three hours earlier—except to shout down commands or suggestions as they'd climbed. He'd seemed subdued. But could she blame him after what she'd said?

When she'd taken a short drink, she handed it back. Stretching her cramped arms above her head, she sighed, feeling a rush of satisfaction with her climb so far. "Yes, I'm pooped—but isn't it a glorious day!"

After stuffing the bottle inside his wind suit, Quaid turned back, his expression softening in a half smile. "You're doing great, Val. How's your hand?"

"Cramp's better." She flexed her fingers. "Just give me five minutes to rest and I'll be as good as new."

"No problem. I can use a breather, too. It's been a long time since I've done this."

"Why don't you breathe a little hard. You'd sound more convincing."

With a pleasant twist of his lips, he stretched out his long legs. The toe spikes of his crampons glistened with ice crystals. Without conscious thought, Val's eyes trailed back up his athletic legs. When she realized where her gaze was lingering, she averted her eyes, not caring to dwell on the all-male shape he displayed.

Even though she'd had to focus her energies on climbing the ice route, she hadn't quite been able to forget her near sexual lapse this morning. And what was worse, every time she'd looked up at him for direction or reassurance, she'd come face-to-face—well, not *face*, exactly—she'd had to stare directly at a pair of extremely appealing male hips. Understandably it had been difficult at times to remember his instructions.

"Val?" She heard his questioning voice.

Abruptly turning toward him, she asked, "Yes—what?"

"I asked if you want to be lead hog on this final pitch?"

"Me?" She swiveled around to get a better look at his face. He was no longer smiling, and appeared to be totally serious. "You mean," she pointed hesitantly toward the sky. "Me—*up there?*"

The brow he lifted was a barely perceptible challenge. "It'd give you experience placing an ice screw or two."

"But I could kill us both."

"Not likely." He tugged on the safety rope, and she could hear the jingle of the carabiners that were snapped to his previously placed screws. "Mine'll hold."

Faced with his dubious faith in her, she gave him a scornful look. "You think mine wouldn't?"

"We'll never know unless you try, now will we?"

With his rather uncomfortable point made, she looked off into the distance where thirty or forty other climbers were ascending various shimmering pillars of ice, oblivious to her mental turmoil. Peering down over the tongue of rock, she calculated that two-hundred-and-some-odd feet was entirely too far from the ground for her to change her mind about the whole project. Besides, what was another fifty feet? So what if there were no safety ropes above her—just frozen, vertical ice? Was that a reason to chicken out now? She closed her eyes and leaned dejectedly against the stone. "Give me two more minutes?"

"Deal," he replied. Even with her eyes closed, she could hear the satisfaction in his voice. Damned if he wasn't going to make a better climber out of her, in spite of herself.

"Quaid," she asked, changing the subject for the next two minutes, at least. "How did a high-powered corporate raider ever get into ice climbing? I'd think you'd go in more for polo or racing cars."

His chuckle was deep and pleasant, so much so that she had to look over at his profile, damaged, yet terribly attractive. Just as quickly, she turned away.

"Ross got me into it. He invited me up here—must have been eight years ago—slapped some crampons on my boots, pointed up the ice and said, 'Let's do it, buddy.'" Bending one knee, Quaid casually settled an arm across it. "I thought the guy's marbles had jumped ship."

"That's a terrible metaphor, but I get it." She turned back to look at him. How broad and masculine he looked in his black wind suit. To distract herself from such foolish thoughts, she hurried on, "So if you thought he was crazy, why did you do it?"

"Ross told me his doctor recommended ice climbing for people with high-stress jobs. Of course he also told me that Ross was the only patient who'd ever taken him up on it."

With his slow grin, Val found herself returning the smile as he went on, "Once I got a taste of it, I found ice climbing to be a release, a way to separate myself from everything but the thrill of finding my edge and seeing how close I could come to it."

She pulled both feet up, the spiked crampons scraping across the frozen stone. "Yes..." She sighed, adding just above a whisper, "It's a good way to escape from the world...."

He glanced down at her. "Is that why you started climbing after your husband died? To escape the grief?"

She shuddered, but not with the cold. Narrowed eyes flicked to meet his and then bounded fretfully away. "That's a pretty personal question."

Wishing her remark hadn't come out so palpably sad, she stiffly gathered up her ice tools and secured the wrist loops about her gloved hands. "Maybe we'd better change the subject. Any last advice?"

"I'm an insensitive ass, Val," he murmured, handing her the coiled bungie cord, ice screws and carabiners. "Sorry..."

She stood, ducking under an overhang as she began to edge toward the ice sheet that was to be their route upward.

She'd doggedly avoided his gaze, hoping he couldn't read the guilt that she knew was in her eyes. *Dammit.* How could she tell him—tell anyone—why she'd started climbing. How could she tell anyone she'd spent four years watching John wither away and that she'd been helpless to comfort him. At least climbing gave her a degree of control over her life, her fear. And with every challenge she met, she felt a little better about herself, a little stronger. One day, perhaps, she might even be able to forgive herself for failing John.

"One piece of advice," she heard Quaid say, surprised at how close he was to her.

She forced herself to face him, forced herself not to be affected by his towering nearness. "What's that?"

"The leader mustn't fall. It's a rule." He grinned down at her. Actually grinned. She could feel the warmth of it all the way to her toes.

Suddenly she forgot her unhappiness, and she grinned back. "Well—as long as it's a rule."

With that, Val leaned out past a long, frail icicle to the more stable ice beyond and planted a pick firmly before swinging out. Jamming the points of her crampons into the ice, she started front-pointing up the glistening wall.

"I'd fire in a screw up another fifteen feet."

"Hush up, down there. Who's the lead hog here? As second man on the rope, your job is to watch my tail," she called back, feeling suddenly very good about this chance to be "at the sharp end of the rope."

"I've created a mouthy monster," he called through a chuckle. "As for keeping an eye on your tail, that's my first priority."

Val felt a rush of embarrassment, realizing that Quaid would be staring up at her backside for the next half hour or so. Preferring not to dwell on it, she called back flippantly, "I bet you say that to all the lead hogs."

There was silence. The high whistle of cold wind across the uneven, shining monolith was all Val could hear. After a long moment, Quaid responded with a subdued, "I haven't had a lead hog in a lot of years, but if I remember right, the second man's job is to watch his leader's butt."

She felt ashamed of herself. Of course, an expert climber such as Quaid, who'd achieved the special prestige of making dozens of first ascents, would have attained a position in the ice climbers' pecking order that would virtually require that he be lead hog at all costs. It dawned on her that he was making quite a concession by giving her this chance to lead.

Smiling sadly to herself, she concentrated on the grueling effort ahead of her. After she'd hammered in a screw and clipped the rope trailing from her harness through the carabiner, she called down, "How was that?"

He merely nodded his approval, making no remarks or suggestions. She gathered from that silent vote of confidence that she was doing fine, and she felt a thrill at her new-found success—however plodding.

It was at thirty feet from the top that her troubles began. Being in the lead position had forced Val to sharpen her concentration and had taken her mind off her fatigue for a time. But now, after twisting in her second ice screw, the cramps in her hands were so severe that she could barely hold on to her ice tools, let alone squeeze open the gate of a carabiner.

Gasping for air, Val dug her front points into the ice and dropped her heels, giving her quivering arms as much rest as possible. Even in the freezing temperature, she could feel sweat trickle between her breasts beneath her lemon-yellow wind suit. She was thoroughly spent, physically and mentally, unable to go on.

With her teeth gritted against the pain in her arms,

she called weakly to Quaid, "I—I'm in a little trouble up here...."

Quaid, waiting at their last belay point, had been aware that she was in trouble for the past several minutes, and he'd been trying to decide the best way to assist her.

He had several options. One was for them to give up and rappel down. Another was for him to untie and free-solo up to her, but he'd be completely without protection. Glancing hesitantly down, he could feel sweat bead on his face despite the cold wind. He wasn't ready to free-solo. It was a cowardly thing to have to admit, but it was the truth.

By the time Val had admitted to her fatigue, Quaid had already decided on the best method of helping her—one that left him with a safety system and allowed her to finish the climb as lead hog.

He smiled up at her, trying to cheer her up, calling, "You're doing great, Val. Tell me. Do you think you could twist in an extra screw where you are?"

She closed her eyes. He could see that wasn't an idea that sat well. He knew she was terribly tired, and twisting another screw into solid ice would be torture for her aching muscles.

"It's the fastest way," he urged. "Then you clip into them and hang and rest." His grin was calculated to be encouraging. "What do you say?" He wasn't going to tell her the whole plan until she was anchored securely and ready to hear it.

With her reluctant nod, he watched as she hammered and twisted a second ice screw into the gleaming surface.

"Okay—now what?" she called down, her voice less than steady. Maybe she had an inkling already of what was coming.

"I'm going to take out my anchor and come up."

He saw panic widen her eyes. "But I'll be unprotected. What if I fall!"

He shook his head. "Don't you trust the screws you just set? That's your anchor. I wouldn't let you be in danger."

She frowned for a minute and then turned back toward the ice and hung listlessly in her harness. "Okay—come on up. I'm on belay—I hope."

He heard her, and his heart went out to her. She thought she'd failed. She wouldn't think that when the day was over, he vowed.

Quickly he took out the anchor screws where he'd been on belay. He swung out on powerful arms and began to front-point up the ice toward her, removing her screws as he advanced. It was the longest, most painful fifteen minutes of Val's life as she waited for him to rescue her. She felt lousy, never realizing how demoralizing it could be to be rescued. How did damsels in distress stand the humiliation?

She'd endured what felt like an eternity of throbbing pain in her cramped arms and hands. Suddenly Quaid's legs were braced on either side of her, and she was engulfed with shame. She knew how utterly she'd failed when she heard him snap two carabiners, securing himself to her screws.

"I hate myself, Quaid...."

"We'll just wait here for a minute. You'll be fine," he assured her in a whisper that was only slightly winded.

Quaid seemed to be all around her, with the full length of him pressing against her back and his legs anchored on either side of her body. With both of their harnesses secured to the same two screws, they were forced into extremely close contact—groin to hip.

"Flex your fingers, Val, and relax. We're almost there."

She couldn't look at him. Instead she stared at the blue-green glaze that was mere inches from her face. Obediently she flexed her fingers.

"Better?" he asked, near her ear.

Groaning, she admitted, "I feel like such a wash-out."

"Why?"

Lifting her unhappy gaze to meet his in spite of her resolve not to, she mumbled, "Because I didn't make it to the top."

He frowned in question, "Do you plan for us to stay here until the spring thaw?"

She blanched. Not just from the unexpected question, but because his lips had grazed her forehead when he'd spoken. They were entirely too close for her peace of mind. She tried to ignore the fact that she was very intimately caught against this man's wildly masculine body. It didn't work. "No, of course I don't plan to stay here. I just mean—"

"I know what you meant," he interrupted softly. "Work that other arm for a minute, then get the hell on up this sucker. I'm getting hungry."

His words were the softest, gentlest command she'd ever heard. When she didn't speak for a minute, he lifted a half grin. "Are you going to flex that left arm or not?"

Obediently she did. "Feels better."

"Naturally."

"How about you? Are you ready?"

His chuckle was oddly wistful. "You could say that." With a jerk of his head he indicated the summit. "I'd take it as a personal favor if you'd get off my lap and show me you can beat this slab of ice."

Her eyes met his gaze, and for one fragile instant, she saw his exposed need—so easy to read, so frightening yet so intoxicating.

A thrill of forbidden desire rushed up her spine, and she found herself wanting to know how those hard, full lips would feel against hers—to know how well he could warm them at this dizzying, frigid height. She too knew a raw need, she realized, the need for another human being's warmth. She'd had years of celibacy and loneliness, and she was only human....

But as his redolent breath teased her lips, her conscience snapped her back to reality with the vile reminder, *You don't deserve any man's warmth. How loving and understanding were you when John needed you?*

The truth hurt—hurt badly. With a reluctance that was almost overwhelming, Val turned away from his gentle bedeviling gaze and untied. With unnecessary force, she swung her ice pick, biting deep into the frozen surface before pulling herself up, away from the stimulating refuge of Quaid's body.

SLIM DISHED OUT a healthy helping of steamed salmon and ambled over to seat himself at Val's kitchen table. "So you actually took the lead today?" he asked as he dribbled egg sauce over his fish.

"Yes. And I soaked in a hot tub for three solid hours when I got home. I can barely lift my arms."

Quaid nodded and smiled a quiet smile. "And tomorrow she's going to tackle Boot Hill."

Val grimaced. "Charming name. Don't they have any waterfalls called Tiny Tot's Trail or Bert and Ernie's Incline? I'm not sure my arms'll be up to anything called Boot Hill by tomorrow."

Slim guffawed. "Oh, come on, Val. You're lovin' every minute of it. How many times have I heard you say you're gonna be the first damned woman up ol' Death Scream?''

Val saw Quaid's fork falter inches from his mouth. She cast a timid glance his way to gauge his reaction to the mention of the ice fall that had almost taken his life. Much to her relief, he took the bite of salmon and continued to eat as though he weren't the least bit affected. Maybe it had been her imagination.

Turning her attention back to Slim, she retorted, "I was nuts." After today, she realized she had a long way to go before attempting such a huge and steep route. "Punch me if I ever mention it again."

"Sure," Slim put in. "That's what you say now. But you'll be harpin' on climbin' Death Scream again this summer, drivin' Mazie and me crazy." Wiping his mustache free of sauce, he asked Quaid, "Say, could you take her up that damned thing this year and give us all a break? And the sooner the better."

Quaid looked up now, his face somber. "Death Scream has never been climbed. I'm not sure Val would want to attempt it, yet."

Slim suddenly frowned as though he just realized whom he was talking to and about what. "Aw, hell." He dropped his napkin on the table, disgusted with himself. "I'm as sorry as I can be, Quaid. I forgot about your damned accident on that piece of sh—ice."

Quaid managed a small smile. "Forget it." Sitting back in his chair, he turned to Val. "I've been wondering how you became a helicopter pilot."

She felt his uneasiness radiate across the table. It was polite of him to express an interest, considering her profession was connected with a time in his life that he clearly wanted to forget. Toying with her cup, she met his gaze. She'd heard the question a hundred times before, so she had the story down to a very few sentences.

For Quaid's sake, she'd make it quick. "My aunt and uncle took me in after the 1964 earthquake—my folks were killed. Uncle Joe was one of Alaska's chopper pilot pioneers—practically invented seat-of-the-pants bush flying. He taught me everything he knew. When he died, I took over the business."

"And you've never wanted to do anything else?"

She took a sip of her coffee. "What you mean is, 'What's a nice girl like me doing in a place like this?'"

Lifting his mug, he observed her over the rim for a moment before he offered, "Not at all. You seem to fit in perfectly here. Sometimes, though, when a person takes over the family business, they can be dissatisfied. I'm happy for you if you're not."

She got up and went to the kitchen counter. "Anybody want more coffee?"

"Not me," called Slim. "But once again, it's the best durned coffee north of the Strait of Juan de Fuca." His mustache lifted in a grin as he turned toward Quaid. "And she's a durned fine pilot, too. She's made some hairy rescues."

"I know," Quaid remarked quietly. "I was one of them." The only evidence that he was distressed was the fact that he glanced away for a moment.

"Hell," Slim groused. "Where's my mind. I knew that. My only excuse is it's been awhile. Sorry, Quaid."

He shrugged, appearing unconcerned.

"Say, Quaid," Val broke in, not wanting to digress into such topics as Quaid's accident, considering how uncomfortable he was with the subject. "Speaking of professions, how does one go from being a corporate raider to a wildlife specialist?"

"It's not hard," he said, clearing away his dishes to have something to do. "The only requirements for studying bears are a warm body and the ability to sit long hours and record their behavior. I've had to work on my handwriting, though." He grinned sheepishly. "No secretary."

"Speaking of secretaries," Slim interjected, jumping up. "I forgot! Mazie nagged me to tell you folks to come into town to the Sundog Club. Seems they got goin' a little party to get the out-a-town ice climbers to mingle and mix with the locals. Since Mazie's brother runs the Sundog, naturally she thinks Val and me oughta show our butts."

"Quaintly put," Val murmured. "Not that I'm exhausted or anything." She ran a hand through her freshly washed hair and exhaled tiredly. "But she is my secretary. I suppose I must put in an appearance...."

Turning to Quaid, Slim added, "She expects your butt there, too, Quaid."

Val couldn't help but laugh. "You can't turn down an invitation worded so charmingly. I'll just go change out of my sweats—be a minute."

"Are you going to wear my favorite red sweater?" Slim queried through an evil chortle.

"Shut up," she shot back.

"Red sweater?" Quaid asked after she'd made her hurried exit.

Slim's mustache twitched wickedly. "If you ever see Val in it, friend, you won't need to ask nothin' more."

"Oh." Nodding in understanding, Quaid turned away to run hot water over the dinner dishes. He hoped to hell she didn't wear her red sweater. It had been a hard enough day as it was.

5

NESTLED BETWEEN a sheltering arm of Prince William Sound and the dramatic mile-high peaks of the Chugach range, Valdez wore a winter-white mantle of deep snow that twinkled like royal finery beneath the city lights.

Slim turned down a wide snow-cleared street and pulled up in front of the rustic Sundog Club. An Olivia Newton-John hit could be heard blasting through the open door as a couple entered ahead of them.

"'Xanadu'?" Quaid asked, taking Val's arm to help her across the slick sidewalk.

Her lips lifted impishly at his incredulous tone. "Marv's a real Olivia Newton-John fan—plays at least half a dozen of her songs every hour."

Quaid chuckled softly. He pulled open the club door and the music hit them head-on as they entered.

"I'll go dig up Mazie," Slim yelled. "She's probably saved us a good table near the stage."

The place was dark, devoid of luxuries and packed with laughing people clad in jeans, sweaters and scuffed boots. Though the club was smoky and over-warm, the customers were a happy, independent crowd. Locals and strangers mingled, united by their passion for ice climbing. They were all here in Valdez to indulge themselves in a two-week climbing frenzy.

Val stood rather uncomfortably beside Quaid in the narrow hallway. His after-shave drifted over her, and she inhaled the scent almost greedily, which was ironic considering how reluctant she was to be standing near him. Needing to move, she suggested, "Let's go on in. Mazie'll find us."

"Come here often?" Quaid shouted as he put a hand to her back to guide her into the milling mob.

Stiffening, she moved imperceptibly away from his touch. "Never—except by threat of death—which is pretty much the way Mazie phrases every request."

They reached the club's main room. With a half laugh, Quaid said, "I thought a nightclub tucked away in remote Alaska would have stuffed moose heads or giant salmon hanging on the walls—not Olivia Newton-John memorabilia."

Everywhere they looked there were Olivia Newton-John posters, album covers and odd, assorted articles of clothing purported to have been worn by the singing star.

"When Marv, Mazie's brother, was in the navy, he went to one of Olivia's shows in L.A. It seems that when she gave him her autograph, she kissed him on the tip of his nose. As you can see, he never recovered from the experience."

"Well! *Hell*, Quaid!" roared a newcomer. "I've been wondering what happened to you since I sent you to Val's place. Figured you'd have given me a buzz by now."

Val and Quaid had been waylaid by a tall, wiry man in his early forties. His thin hawkish face was animated with delight. "Where you been keeping yourself?"

"Actually, Ross," Val called over the noise, "my dog chewed the phone cord, and I haven't had time to get it fixed."

Ross Knox nodded expansively and put a friendly hand on her shoulder. "Billy Bob strikes again, huh?"

He turned and winked at Quaid. "You met her puppy from hell?"

Quaid shook his head at his friend. "You think you're funny, don't you? Why didn't you tell me Val was a woman—with a wolf for a guardian angel?"

Ross frowned in thought. "Didn't I tell you she was a woman?"

Val interjected. "Oh, Ross probably didn't think of it. I'm just one of the guys around here. Right, Ross?"

The older man gave her a smile that was somehow poignant. "Wouldn't have it any other way."

"Hey, Val!" bellowed a burly man from the other end of the room. He was winding his way toward her as he called. "Thanks for the business."

She waved at him. "Hope it helps."

He made it to her side. "Every little bit." Pausing, he grew sober. "Sorry about your chopper. When can it be ready for service?"

Val deftly dodged a scurrying waitress before shouting back, "Next week, I hope. Slim's got the part ordered."

The barrel-chested man nodded and looked over at Quaid for the first time. "Hullo." Sticking out a paw, he introduced himself. "Joe Carter. Chopper pilot. You a climber?"

Taking his proffered hand, Quaid nodded. "Quaid Perrault. I've been out of it awhile, but yes, I climb. You?"

Joe shook his head. "Never tried, but I thought I might give it a shot this year. Say," he turned to Val. "Will ya take a spin on the dance floor with me?"

"I'd love to dance."

"Okay, Val—let's rip up the floor."

Just then, Ricky Nelson's "Be-bop Baby" boomed

over the speaker system, assaulting their ears merci-
lessly, and Joe yelped for joy. "I love this one!"

With some reluctance, Quaid watched her go, then
faced his friend, remarking, "I like your friend, Ross.
Val's generous, kindhearted and, I think, very vulnerable."

Both of Ross's brows jumped upward in surprise. "It
sounds like you've spent some time thinking about it."

"And from that sorry smile you gave her awhile ago,
I'd say you have, too."

The older man flinched. Dropping his gaze, he
cocked his head toward a dark corner. "Let's get a table."

Once they were seated, Ross confided, "Lots of men
in this town have thought about it. But Val has made it
clear that she's not interested. She's one of those
women who can't get over her husband's death." He
beckoned a waitress, adding, "She just doesn't want to
have anything to do with another man. It's sad. She's a
hell of a woman, but vulnerable? That's bull. Val is one
totally together woman. She's an ace chopper pilot,
she's a damned salty ice climber, and she tells you exactly where you stand. Vulnerable, hell!"

As the waitress took their orders, Quaid glanced toward the dance floor. He could catch fleeting glimpses
of Val as she swayed and shimmied to and fro in
rhythm to yet another Olivia Newton-John offering.
Frowning in thought, he wondered if Ross's interpre-
tation was wholly correct. Was it grief that kept Val at
arm's length from men, or was it something more? He
had the nagging feeling that she was fighting some awful internal battle. Watching her dance, seeing her
friendly yet aloof demeanor with her gawky partner,
he became convinced that there was something gnawing at her. He didn't know what it was, but because he

liked his spirited little hostess he wanted her to be happy.

Rubbing a hand over his face, he felt his eye patch, and he faltered at the reminder of his broken countenance. Casting his self-pitying thoughts away, he made a silent vow to do what he could to help rid Val of her own scars—unseen, though very real—whatever they might be.

When their drinks came, Ross stuffed a pill into his mouth and downed it with a draught of cold beer.

"What's the matter?" Quaid asked, sipping his cola.

"Headache." Ross dismissed it with a broad wave to indicate the room. "The noise in this place breeds 'em like shrimp."

Quaid's grin was sardonic. "Or Olivia Newton-John tunes."

Ross burst out laughing. "Too true. Maybe I'm getting too old for this."

Quaid eyed his friend seriously. "You look a little pale. You sure you're okay?"

"Hell," Ross shot back with a laugh. "You don't look like any pinup in this light, either, bub."

"Oh? It's the light in *here* that makes me look like this." Quaid lifted an ironic brow. "That takes a load off my mind."

Ross's glance rose hastily to meet his friend's cynical gaze, and he made an apologetic face. "Hey, man, you know I didn't mean—"

"Forget it," Quaid insisted, hiding his annoyance with himself for allowing the offhand remark to bother him.

Val was suddenly there, laughing and bidding a stranger goodbye. Quaid noted a bit irritably that her new escort was a hulking Adonis with perfect teeth—

and *two* eyes. Taking a big gulp of his drink, Quaid politely stood.

The young Schwarzenegger-type ambled off. "Mind if I join you two?" Val asked a little breathlessly. "Slim's found an admirer, and Mazie's already gone. It seems her kids ganged up on the baby-sitter, and now the poor woman's threatening to sue for mental cruelty or something."

"I thought that was just in divorces," Ross interjected as he rose belatedly to his feet.

"Mazie's kids may set new judicial precedents."

A ghost of a smile flitted across Quaid's lips. "Your secretary lives a full life."

He motioned toward a rushing waitress. "What will you have to drink, Val?"

"Orange juice with lots of ice, thanks."

Just as Quaid placed her order, a squat, freckled man with an inner tube of fat around his middle, stepped up onto a small stage in the corner of the room. A garish red spotlight hit him, giving his jowly face the look of a man who's just pulled his head from a steaming lobster pot.

His grin was friendly, though, as his nasal twang boomed into the microphone. "Evenin' folks and welcome to 'Marv's Mixer' for all you crazy ice-climbin' fools." There was a titter of laughter and a few raunchy remarks as he held up his hand for silence. "But seriously—Big Marv wants to get you really *mixed* now with one of the Sundog's favorite mix-'em-up games." He paused for emphasis. "The Olivia Newton-John Shuffle!"

When a low rumble of good-natured moaning and mumbling swept through the room, Quaid leaned closer to Val and whispered, "Is the Olivia Newton-John Shuffle anything like the bunny hop?"

She shook her head, but before she could spell out the details, Marv was trumpeting his own explanation. "Grab yourself a partner and get your numb butts up on the dance floor and trip the light fantastic. When I stop Olivia's song, you change partners. If you don't have a new—and I mean *new* partner when Olivia starts to warble her sweet notes again, you're out. Everybody got it?"

"*Hell*, Marv, we're not morons!" Ross shouted, laughing.

"That's debatable, Rosco old man!" Marv shouted back to hoots of laughter. "Okay, if the kibitzing is over, let's get this show on the road."

Ross leaned across the table. "May I have the honor of dragging your numb butt across the dance floor, Mrs. Larrabee?"

She granted him an excessively gracious smile. "Why, Mr. Knox—how could I turn down such a gallant petition."

In a quick aside to Quaid, he said, "You gotta know how to talk to 'em."

"Excuse me, Mr. Perrault?"

Quaid looked up. A young, slender woman in a lacy blouse and cord slacks was smiling tentatively down at him. "You probably don't remember me, but we met— er—the last time you were in town." She held out her hand. "I'm Agnes Abels. I don't climb, but I just *love* climbers. I was a waitress over in the—"

"Pipeline Club," Quaid finished for her as he stood, taking her hand in his. "Hello, Agnes. How've you been?"

She blushed. "Married and divorced, but I'm fine. I work over at the United Way office now. Secretary." Licking her chapped lips, she asked, "I was wondering if you'd dance with me?"

Quaid hadn't danced in years, and he had no desire to do so. But he could tell that Agnes had had to work up her courage to ask him, so he couldn't bring himself to refuse. "I'd be honored, Agnes," he lied. With a grin he didn't feel, he placed a hand at her elbow and eased her through the crowd. "You'll have to forgive me. I'm pretty rusty."

She glanced bashfully over at him. "Nobody who could dance as well as you used to could be all that bad."

They'd reached the crowded floor and Olivia had just begun to croon "Have You Never Been Mellow?" Obligingly, Quaid took Agnes into his arms and they moved smoothly along the floor. Agnes placed her face against Quaid's chest. Surprised, he looked down at the top of her tightly permed head.

"I'm real sorry about your eye, Mr. Perrault," she murmured against his flannel shirt.

He was accustomed to the remark by now and let it slide. "Call me Quaid."

She looked up, but kept her cheek pressed to his chest. "You know, I'm here with a couple of my girl-friends, and they think the patch doesn't really hurt your looks that much. You look kinda like a pirate. Scary but sexy, you know?"

He was at a loss. Fortunately Olivia went quiet—a double blessing. "I think we have to change partners, Agnes," he reminded her, grateful for Marv's timing.

She frowned. "Well, maybe later?" Her expression was hopeful, pitifully so, as someone caught Quaid's hand and drew his attention. A chubby woman pulled him to her buxom breast and shouted, "Boy, I almost missed you. I've won this contest a couple of times. Marv gives away great stuff. I got a twenty-five-dollar Frederick's of Hollywood gift certificate last time.

Bought a peekaboo bra. My name's Ginger." She paused in her recital long enough to look up in his face and her eyes widened. "Wow, mister, what happened to—" She stopped herself, but her shocked expression said it all.

The music stopped again and Ginger dashed off. Fortunately Quaid had no time to linger on her unfinished question. Immediately he was grabbed by another partner.

It went on like that for three of Olivia's seemingly endless hits. Finally, when Quaid was about to decide to skulk silently from the dance floor, he found himself face-to-face with Val. She appeared just as startled by their chance encounter as he.

The music began, and to Val's dismay, not only was Quaid taking her into his arms, but the song, "Physical," began. Its lyrics held decidedly suggestive overtones—no, now that she listened carefully, she was distressed to realize that they were blatant, throaty demands to be made love to. Val swallowed and cast a quick, unhappy glance at Quaid's face. There was just the merest smile trailing across his lips. Rats! She didn't need this. Inwardly she prayed that Marv would make this unfortunate captivity within Quaid's arms a short one.

Deciding she should at least acknowledge him, she said, "Hi…"

His smile broadened. "Hello, buddy."

"Having fun?"

"I am now."

She cast her gaze away. Her mutinous body was entirely too aware of his hips and thighs crushed against hers. "We really could be dancing apart. This isn't that slow a song."

"I never mastered dancing that way. Sorry."

She swallowed again. *Well, you've certainly mastered dancing this way!* her mind roared. But all she actually said was, "Oh…well…no problem."

He held her close, swaying and rocking so suavely and seductively she could almost imagine they were lying prone in a hammock. Distressed, she began to feel an urgent need to lie beneath this man, to let him sway and rock over her until he carried her to a lover's paradise—something her woman's instincts screamed that he could accomplish quite expertly.

With a faulty sigh, she cast a pained glance toward Marv. He was engaged in what appeared to be a thorough grope of his current girlfriend. Apparently the tune, "Physical," held some evil power over Marv's free will, keeping his hand far from the stereo's needle.

Stop the damned music, Marv! she shrieked telepathically. But Olivia kept right on lamenting how hard a time she was having keeping herself from ripping some man's clothes off. Poor Olivia! Without doubt, she too had been forced to dance hip to hip, thigh to thigh and chest to breast with Quaid Perrault at some fragile point in her emotional life. The experience was enough to move any woman to a life-threatening shortness of breath and an urge to beg for ultimate release.

"You know," she heard Quaid murmur into her hair, "this song grows on you."

She gritted her teeth. Any answer at this point would be incriminating.

With his hand at the small of her back, pressing her into him, he did another one of his hip grinds, and she bit off a wail of protest. At her first opportunity, she was going to kill Marv!

"What's tonight's prize?" Quaid asked, drawing her back to the problem at hand.

"I—I don't know." She cleared her husky voice. "If Marv announced it beforehand, nobody'd dance."

Quaid's chuckle not only tickled her cheek, but her breasts. "What? Don't you want a Frederick's of Hollywood gift certificate?"

Her lips wavered in an uncertain smile in spite of her dismal mood. "So, you danced with Ginger."

"Uh-huh," he affirmed. "She bought—"

"I know what Ginger bought," Val all but snapped. Her nerves were bound so tightly she wanted to scream. "Her husband likes that sort of thing."

"Most husbands would."

"I couldn't care less...." she mumbled, her resentment rising to explosive levels. First Quaid turned her on, completely against all her desires on the subject, then he proceeded to bring up the hurtful subject of husbands and their erotic appetites. She was sure Quaid would be appalled if he knew how John had reacted to her sexual overtures after he'd discovered he was ill—how he'd rejected any physical relationship with her, leaving her bereft, unfulfilled and resentful. Unthinking, she blurted, "Some husbands might not be... *Oh*, mind your own business!"

The music stopped, and she yanked out of his embrace. The silence that surrounded them was thick and deadly. For an infinitesimal moment it seemed as though Quaid were staring directly into her soul. "There's more to your problem with John than just grief, isn't there, Val?"

His indictment, though just above a whisper, seemed deafening in the stillness of the room. Val's jaw went slack in her shock, and she felt as though he'd slapped her. Before she could cry out her defensive denial, she was whirled away in another man's arms.

6

THE OLIVIA NEWTON-JOHN SHUFFLE was long over, and much to Val's surprise, Quaid had won, along with the aggressive, enthusiastic Ginger.

Ginger came by the table for the second time to show off her half of the prize—double cassette tapes entitled, "Horacio Marwood Yodels His Greatest Hits." She was ecstatic about her award, which was nothing short of a miracle. While she chattered away, Val painted on a smile and wondered idly what horrid travesty of taste Quaid had won.

As the evening plodded slowly along, Val tried to appear cheerful, but she was growing more and more upset. Every muscle in her upper body was screaming in pain. She wanted to go home and go to bed, even though it was just past ten o'clock. Still, if she was to be honest with herself, it wasn't so much sore muscles that was disturbing her. It was Quaid—and the confused way she'd reacted to him on the dance floor. Her body still tingled from the experience, and she'd been expending far too much energy trying to convince herself that the feeling was some odd form of animosity.

Glancing around, she caught sight of him, head and shoulders above the crowd, holding some curly-coiffed female within his embrace. He'd been dancing with one giggly young woman or another ever since the contest ended. Ross had finally taken pity on Quaid and relieved him of his garishly wrapped prize, which, she noted dolefully, he hadn't had time to open. He hadn't even been back to the table!

Clearly his swarthy, pirate looks were an appealing draw. Somehow, though she didn't like to admit it, she couldn't blame the women who had been clamoring to dance with him. He was an exceedingly sexual animal when he moved around the dance floor. His physical mastery out there, swaying in close contact with some simpering young woman, was sinful to watch, let alone participate in.

Well… she reminded herself silently, *the state of his dance card isn't my business.*

Surreptitiously she gazed toward the dance floor again and was surprised to see Quaid ambling toward her and Ross. She swallowed, her thoughts jumping waywardly to how wonderfully he probably made love. Though she'd danced with the man for only a few minutes, she knew in the depths of her soul that he would be even more marvelous in bed.

With an abruptness she didn't expect, Quaid snagged her gaze and smiled down at her. She hadn't realized she was openly watching his approach and was embarrassed to discover that she had been. With every fiber of her being, she hoped he had no idea along what lewd path her mind had been trekking.

When he reached their table, he sat down next to her. Reluctantly she noted the economy and unconscious grace of his movements. When their knees unexpectedly brushed, Val moved away, hesitant to make any further physical contact with him.

Quaid noticed her withdrawal and cursed himself inwardly. Outwardly he flashed a tired grin. "I don't know about you folks," he began. "But I'm bushed. Do you think we'd offend Mazie if we left?"

"I'll never tell. I'm dead on my feet." Val said. "Do you think Slim's ready?"

"I think he's going to be busy," Quaid offered vaguely.

"For a man who looks like an emaciated walrus, that guy does pretty well with the ladies," Ross interjected, shaking his head.

"He's just not as discriminating as you are, Ross." Val gave her friend a gentle pinch on his cheek. "If you'd quit hanging around with us guys, you might do better."

Ross chuckled, but with little conviction. "Don't worry about me. The night's young." When Val and Quaid stood, he followed suit. "Will I see you two tomorrow?"

"Let's make a climb together," Val suggested. "I may have a tough time of it without the use of my arms."

"It's a date."

"Boot Hill okay?" Quaid asked. "That was my plan."

Ross's eyes sparkled with enthusiasm. "That's one slippery piece of real estate."

"You don't have to go," Val chided, egging him on. "If you can't take a little challenge...."

"You're the one with the burning arms," Ross reminded her with a mild squeeze of her forearm.

She winched. "Ugly rumor. Ten o'clock?"

"I'll be there."

With that, Quaid led Val through the jumble of tables toward the exit. It took all of her willpower not to dwell on the fact that his coaxing fingers were gentle and warm at her back. Another thought struck her and struck her hard, as they went out into the snowy night. Why was life so fickle and unfair? The very last person

she wanted to be alone with right now was Quaid Perrault…and she was going *home* with him!

BY THURSDAY, Quaid could tell that Val felt much better—at least where her muscles were concerned. With
Quaid and Ross as her teachers, she'd progressed by
leaps and bounds, bolstering both her confidence and
her craving to climb the more demanding routes.

On the down side, she'd completely retreated from
him. She'd been civil and tremendously hardworking
on the ice. But she'd distanced herself emotionally after
that night at the club. She wasn't a woman who relin-
quished her private troubles easily.

Quaid had been treading lightly, trying to repair
their relationship—make her comfortable around him
again. Though he'd come to Valdez with a need to beat
Death Scream, these past four days of watching Val
present a fearless face to the world had touched something in him. He could read her as easily as he could
read a brown bear, and he saw pain, ugly, gnawing
pain, in her eyes.

He knew he was becoming entirely too drawn to Val
and he should back off. It was a deadly mistake to be
distracted from his purpose with worries over a
woman. He'd lost the use of one eye and almost his life
learning that lesson.

Yet he could see that the very strength and resolve
Val worked so hard to show the world was her way of
masking a formidable insecurity. Just what that was,
he couldn't imagine. His need to help Val defeat her
unhappy secret was becoming as strong in him as his
need to defeat Death Scream—not a good develop-
ment since he needed tremendous concentration to attempt to climb the killer falls.

Once again, as he had been four years ago, before his

fall, he was at war within himself. But he couldn't help it. As much as he wanted to push her away, he needed to draw her closer. He found himself walking an emotional tightrope, and he was beginning to wonder if this time his combative compulsions would end in his death.

FRIDAY MORNING BROUGHT a bright new day, along with a bizarre addition to Valdez's celebration of the ice-climbing festival—the Iceworm Parade and dinner dance. This would be a time of rest and revelry for the climbers as they kicked their crampons and ice tools into some dark corner and spent the day honoring the noble iceworm.

Val hung up her newly repaired phone and turned toward the kitchen where Quaid was playing Save the Sock with Billy Bob. "It looks as though you've been recruited," she called over her pet's snarling.

Quaid looked up from his all-four's position, his face a dashing mixture of amusement and frustration. "Who are you talking to?"

"You. Can't you get your sock back?"

Quaid shook his head. "Apparently she's taken a liking to it."

Val fought a grin, not wanting to be drawn into his affable mood. No matter how hard she tried to remain detached from this man, he battered at her wall of reserve at every turn. Right now, watching Quaid, one foot clad in a red wool sock, trying unsuccessfully to rescue the other from her brawling pet, Val was having a hard time keeping a stern hold over her anger and misgivings. Quaid looked so cute and harmless, wheedling and cajoling her dog, who was delighted with the game. She felt a little sorry for her houseguest. He might be a whiz with big brown bears, but he was getting nowhere with her hound.

Planting her hands on her hips, she called out a reprimand. "Billy Bob! You let him have his sock this minute or I'll..." She paused, her mouth working. *What? What exactly was she going to do short of teargassing the mutt?*

"This had better be good," Quaid offered through a chuckle as he gave his sock up for lost. When he let go, the dog fell back on her haunches and began to shake the woolen memento ferociously.

"Okay—okay. You won. Don't rub it in." Sitting back, Quaid pulled off the other sock and dangled it in front of the giant mongrel's snout. "Here, sweetheart, have a ball."

Val straightened her face, retreating behind her reserved pose. "I'm sorry, Quaid. I owe you a new pair."

He pushed up from the floor and, with long, easy strides, made quick work of the stairs to his loft. "It'll keep me up nights." When he'd disappeared from view, he called down to her. "What have I been recruited for?"

"Oh—I'd almost forgotten. As a worm segment in the parade."

He reappeared, his head and shoulders looming out over the railing. "A *what* segment?"

His expression was appealingly bewildered. Against her will, she smiled up at him. "Worm. Remember? I told you if Slim got the hydraulic pump today, he'd have to drop out of the parade to work on my chopper. He just called to tell me the part came in. So, we're missing iceworm segment number twenty-three." She spread her hands contritely. "I hope you don't mind. It'll just be for an hour or two."

He pursed his lips and disappeared again. "What

color socks do iceworm segments wear?" he asked loud enough to be heard from the loft.

"Color is up to the individual segment. I'm wearing yellow."

"You're a segment?"

"Twenty-two."

There was such a long pause that Val assumed Quaid had decided to put an end to the silly conversation. "I'll get our parkas," she called.

Just then he towered at the head of the stairs. Lifting his pant legs so that she could see fluorescent green socks that sported random, mauve splotches and a separate sleeve for each toe, he asked, "Think these will do?"

She stared. Never had she seen such ugly foot gear in her life. "They're…" She struggled to ward off an outright grin. Finally losing out to the whimsical picture he presented, she smiled. "They're awful. Where did you get such a ghastly pair of socks?"

They were grinning at each other now, and Quaid felt a surge of good humor for the first time in days. Wiggling his toes, he replied, "These, my good woman, are just half of my grand prize in the Olivia Newton-John Shuffle. Would you care to see the boxer shorts?"

Her choked response was answer enough. Silently Quaid blessed Marv for his terrible taste. It was good to hear Val laugh again.

"HAVE YOU EVER SEEN ONE?" Quaid asked as they moved forward over the icy street, cloaked within their one-hundred-foot-long replica of an iceworm.

"Seen one what?" she asked, carefully avoiding the heels of the young woman in front of her.

"An iceworm."

"Sure. Haven't you?"

"No. And neither have you. They're a hoax, aren't they?"

She concentrated on watching her feet. Whoever had constructed their huge costume had neglected to give the segments much walking room. "I—er—what was the question?"

"Aren't iceworms a hoax?" he repeated near her ear. She felt an unruly shiver rush up her spine and worked at ignoring it.

"Once, when I was flying out an early skiing charter, I took a swing over Valdez glacier. It was just dawn, and the sun hit the glacier like a spotlight bouncing off a tin roof. They were coating the surface, a carpet of thousands of tiny worms. But a minute after being hit by the light, they'd all burrowed into the glacier's surface. It was eerie. One of the skiers almost lost his breakfast when I told him what he'd just seen."

Quaid chuckled. His warm breath tickled her neck beneath her knit cap. "Maybe some morning I'll charter your copter and you can take me up to see it."

"Okay, but I'm not cheap."

"From what I've seen and heard, you're not even in the damned market."

Val felt a rush of horror at the direction their conversation had abruptly taken. Was he daring to make a comment on her sex life? Forgetting where she was, she spun to confront him. "And just exactly what—" She plowed headlong into his chest, halting further comment.

Outside their undulating fabric worm, spectators were witness to what appeared to be a sudden muscle spasm squarely in the middle of the worm's torso. And then, in a comical display, fifty worm segments toppled one upon another until the once-impressive iceworm was little more than a pulsating strip of canvas and a few stray legs flailing around on the surface of Valdez's ice-coated main street. Shouts of surprise and bewilderment turned to laughter and giggles as entwined bodies began to wriggle to right themselves.

Quaid found himself beneath Val, who was straddling him, her lips temptingly near his. It was peculiarly dark now that the canvas had settled to the ground around them, but there was no mistaking the fact that Val's face was hovering above his own, her arms braced on either side of his shoulders. Her breath was coming in short little pants.

"Are you hurt?" he asked, sounding winded.

"Where are you?" Her question came out in a high-pitched whisper.

"Who do you think you're sitting on?"

"Oh, no," she groaned. "Are *you* hurt?"

He murmured something she couldn't quite understand, and some instinct told her it was just as well.

She started to slide off him, but found the laces of her mukluk caught on something. "I—I can't seem to… Quaid, my boot lace is stuck on your coat."

He pushed them both up to a sitting position, which proved to be a bad mistake; Val ended up straddling his lap in a dangerously intimate fashion. It was so dark he couldn't see what the problem was. "I—just a minute—" He reached for the edge of the canvas but found that it was being held down.

"What the—"

It suddenly dawned on them both that the spectators had joined in the fun by entrapping the fallen fifty beneath their elongated prison.

"This is just fine," he muttered near her cheek, his voice grave with irritation, or was it something else? "I'm sorry, Val."

She'd been yanking on her boot and, with an exasperated sigh, turned to face him. Their lips accidentally brushed and the contact was devastating. Val froze, suddenly paralyzed, lip to lip with Quaid.

The clamor of laughter and voices dimmed and faded away with Quaid's frustrated moan. "Hell, Val..." he murmured, his mouth as soft and welcome against hers as summer sunshine.

Neither one of them had initiated the kiss, it just happened—a reflex like smiling back at a baby's grin. The thrill was the same, too. Pure and sweet...at first.

7

HIS MOUTH BARELY BRUSHED HERS. His kiss was fleeting and short-lived. She could tell he'd thought better of what he had begun and had withdrawn on his own. She'd wanted to believe it had been a mutual withdrawal, with both of them regaining themselves quickly. But she wasn't fooling herself. Her body remained rigid, ready to be kissed a second time, and very regretful of the loss. When his lips brushed hers again, it was without warning, but an answer to her irrational prayer.

With his mouth against hers, Quaid groaned, "Hell—Val…" His tone was self-condemning, but his lips were warm and coaxing. As his mouth, so exquisitely male, slid across hers, Val's lips grew heated, supple, and began to reply in kind.

She'd almost forgotten how a man's lips felt. But he brought it back to her in all its vital beauty. She desperately needed to move away from Quaid, to battle her desire to be held, touched, comforted.

She felt a rush of shame for, with Quaid's kiss, she'd grown weak, losing sight of the terrible truth about herself, her fatal flaw. With her hands pressing against his chest, she tried to put an end to this powerful reminder of what she'd thought she had left behind her. Pushing against him, she resisted with all her might— at least she did so in her mind. Her body defied her command to retreat, and the result was a feeble shove.

Appalled with herself but unable to keep her emotions in check, Val opened her mouth in invitation. She couldn't imagine why she was succumbing now—here in this absurd setting. She only knew there was something undeniable about Quaid....

As she futilely tried to analyze her lapse, his teeth gently nipped at her lower lip and he slid his arms around her, pulling her toward him. His groan spoke volumes as he accepted her wordless enticement to enjoy the honeyed recesses of her mouth. He was eloquent in his unspoken messages, and her body soared with the soft secrets his lips and tongue were divulging.

His large, gentle hands slid beneath her parka to thrill the small of her back with determined yet delicate strokes.

"Oh, Val," he murmured against her mouth. "Why did it have to be here?"

His plea had been spoken huskily and in such a sexually frustrated tone that it sent a shaft of dismay racing through Val, piercing her passion-clouded reason. The reality of what was happening sobered her instantly. Because of her nameless need to know this man more intimately, she had unleashed something not easily quenched. It was all well and good to indulge herself in a moment's frailty, but it was a different matter to give Quaid the idea that she had any intention of moving this crazy thing to its obvious conclusion.

This time, with fear spurring her on, she was able to push Quaid away from her, though she was still nestled familiarly in his lap.

"I—Quaid—please..." She ran a shaky hand across her mouth in a vain attempt to wipe away the reality of his kiss. "I told you I have no intention of getting involved with *any* man."

Only the vague outline of his face was detectable beneath the canvas cover, and she couldn't make out his features beyond the barest well-remembered image. Even so, she knew he wasn't smiling.

It wasn't until Quaid trailed his hands from beneath her parka that Val realized he'd continued to hold her for that last, silent moment. His abandonment was clearly a reluctant one, as was his murmured remark, "I'd hoped you'd decided I wasn't just any man...."

She swallowed, feeling terrible. She'd wanted him to kiss her, and she'd known she should have prevented it. But she hadn't. Damn it all! What was it about this man that made her lose sight of her resolve to avoid entanglements? With her throat closing against a guilty lump, she muttered, "Don't take this personally, Quaid, but it just can't happen between us."

The fact that there were hoots of laughter and animated chatter around them penetrated Val's world again, and she decided that sitting within the all too intimate embrace of Quaid's legs was no way to be found once the canvas was raised.

Strangely fatigued, she gave her captured mukluk another yank to no avail, then asked tiredly, "What have I gotten myself stuck on?"

"Someday you're going to have to figure that out and get on with your life, Val," he stated in a tight whisper. "But right now, let's worry about your foot." To get his bearings in the darkness, he lightly ran his hand down her leg to where her mukluk was attached to his coat.

She fought to ignore his touch, though she could tell his ministrations were totally business at this point. A few more seconds passed before she was free of him.

"My pocket fastener is shaped like an anchor. That's what snagged your boot laces. Sorry." The regret in his voice went beyond the problem of her boot, and Val knew he was regretting much more than he was saying.

She wasted no time in scrambling away. On her hands and knees she assured him, "No real harm done." It had come out only somewhat nonchalant, but better than she had any right to expect. Her timing, it turned out, was perfect, for the canvas lifted and the trapped inhabitants began to clamber to freedom. Val made sure she was among the first to emerge.

Quaid, on the other hand, took quite awhile to crawl out. Modesty required that he wait until the effect of Val's kiss had subsided enough so that the snugness of his jeans gave away nothing of their unfortunate encounter.

USING THE EXCUSE that she wanted to get an early start climbing the next day, Val declined the invitation to attend the dinner dance that evening. The last thing in the world she wanted was another clash with Quaid on the dance floor. Physical contact with the man was lethal, and she wanted no more of it! Quaid thwarted her plan to be rid of him for the evening by agreeing that he too was tired of dances and wanted to get to bed early.

The idea of both of them being in bed early—spending extra hours prone, not very far apart—didn't appeal to her at all. In a final desperate attempt to be separated from Quaid, at least for a time, she told him she really ought to go to the hangar and check on Slim. Her mechanic had planned to stay at work until he had the chopper repaired. When Quaid offered to see if he could be of any help, Val panicked, practically ordering him to go on to the dinner dance.

Ultimately Quaid had to face the fact that Val didn't want him around. In a compromise, he said he'd stay at home and read, then go to bed early and he'd see her in the morning. This idea seemed to sit relatively well with Val, so reluctantly he let her borrow his Jeep and go off alone to the hangar.

He was galled with himself for upsetting her, and while she was gone, he made several calls to the local hotels to see if any rooms had opened up. He knew Val was too kindhearted to throw him out, but he also knew that after this afternoon she was uneasy around him.

She'd made no comment about his remark concerning "getting on with her life," but he knew she'd heard it and she'd been distressed by his probing. He'd been distressed, too, when he'd heard himself make the stupid, uncalled-for remark. But Val's unwillingness to face her problem had been preying on his mind, and he hadn't been able to keep his mouth shut.

Now that he was alone in her house, alone that is but for a mammoth hound whose head rested in his lap, he rebuked himself silently. When would he learn to mind his own business where this woman was concerned?

He'd just climbed into bed when he recalled he hadn't had dinner. Positive he wouldn't be able to sleep anyway, he decided to eat something. Slipping on a pair of sweatpants, he loped down the stairs toward the kitchen and was just about to round the corner when the front door opened.

Val didn't see him until she'd locked herself in and flipped on the entry light. When she finally did notice him, she stumbled to a halt halfway out of her parka.

The single bulb over the door illuminated his contoured chest and long, lean torso. The drawstring waistband of his pants was so low slung on his hips it was practically indecent. The dim, golden glow from the light made him appear flawless as he towered over her, his expression watchful, his stance wary.

And why did the patch on his right eye only serve to accentuate his raw beauty? She stared in awe, wishing she'd never left this evening, wishing she was safely tucked away in her bedroom, unaware of his half-naked midnight prowl.

Quaid grinned affably, an emotion he didn't feel, and broke the awkward silence. "Hi—I have the munchies. Would you like a sandwich or something?"

She regained her composure and slid her parka off. Hanging it on the hook by the door, she admitted, "Sounds good. I forgot to eat this evening."

"Two grilled cheese sandwiches, coming up."

Much to Val's relief, he disappeared into the kitchen, but his half-clad gorgeousness was burned into her mind. Even the sweatpants—a garment that was supposed to promise baggy oblivion—failed to mask Quaid's obvious nakedness beneath the gray fabric.

Something deep in her stomach constricted, and grew painfully warm. *Damn the man!* Was there no end to the torture he could inflict on her just by walking into a room?

She'd remained over in that cold helicopter hangar long after Slim had gone, pacing and ranting, venting her anger and embarrassment over what had happened this afternoon. She'd hoped she'd not only get it out of her system, but that she'd tire herself out so completely that she would be able to do no more than fall, exhausted, into her bed. But now, Quaid had to meet her at the door and remind her not only of the fact that she was hungry for food, but that she was ravenous for the feel of his arms—and legs—about her—*and that she had no right to desire him!*

Several moments later, after splashing some cold water on her face, she'd slipped into her warm fuzzies and reluctantly joined Quaid in the little kitchen. He was flipping the sandwiches on the grill, his back to her. She was a little surprised to note that he'd donned a robe. Considerate of him, she thought, though her teeth remained gritted. Damage had been done, nonetheless.

Affecting her best hostess pose, she joined him at the stove. "Smells good, Quaid. You're quite a cook."

He glanced over at her, his smile halfhearted. "I'm learning." Turning away to flip a sandwich, he added, "Food's about ready. Mind getting the coffee?"

Grateful to have something to do, she shuffled over to the coffeepot. With her back to him, she searched for an unthreatening subject. "Where's Billy Bob?" she queried lightly.

"Sound asleep in my bed."

She blanched. Was there no escaping the subject of his bed? "Oh—I'll get her after we eat."

"You and who else?"

Her lips lifted without mirth. He was probably right. Billy Bob slept where she wanted. Val wished it was that easy for human beings.

Carrying two steaming mugs of coffee, she returned to the table, switching to a totally innocuous subject. "I hope this is decaf. You realize it's after midnight."

"It is." He turned toward the table with a plate in each hand. "And I do."

Once they were seated, Val was at a loss for polite chitchat, so she took a bite of her sandwich.

"How's the copter coming?"

She swallowed. "Fine." For the life of her she couldn't understand why she was suddenly mute. Feeling flushed and tongue-tied, she stared down at her half-eaten sandwich.

There was a long pause. Val nibbled out of nervousness rather than any desire to eat, having lost her appetite for food. She was very aware that Quaid made no sound at all. He wasn't eating. He wasn't sipping coffee. He wasn't even moving. Somehow, she knew that his one, swarthy eye was riveted on her and that his expression was grave.

"Val," he finally ventured, his tone contrite.

Her fidgety gaze darted to meet his. She offered him her brightest smile. It felt stiff and unnatural. "Yes, Quaid?"

His nostrils flared, and Val could see that he was affronted by her pretense. She tried to sip her coffee to appear casual, but her stomach was tied in knots.

Quaid allowed his eye to close for a moment before he looked at her again. He dragged his hand through his hair, loosening strands from the leather strip that held it in place. A few dark locks fell across his forehead, giving him an unexpectedly vulnerable look that was disturbing.

When he finally spoke, his words shocked her. "I tried to get a room in town tonight. They're full up. I'll try again in a few days."

She frowned, and it surprised her to realize that it wasn't because there were no rooms available. It upset her because he *wanted* to leave. "I didn't realize my home fell so short of your standards, Mr. Perrault."

He sat back in his chair, his shoulders sagging in exasperation. "*Hellfire*, you know it isn't that."

She too sat back, crossing her arms before her in an

unconscious, protective move. "I'm afraid I don't. Why not enlighten me."

His ebony gaze swept over her, sparkling with some thwarted emotion. Then, unexpectedly and with a thunderous crash, he slammed his hands on the table, knocking over his chair as he stood. "You know damned well why." Twisting away from her, he stalked across the room. "I kissed you this afternoon. Don't tell me that didn't complicate things."

Lifting her chin, she feigned a coolness she didn't feel. "I've been kissed before." Pushing back from the table, she stood, marching pointedly away from him. "It wasn't the kiss that upset me, Quaid. And I think you know that." She spun to face him. "Don't you, Mr. So-Very-Able-To-Read-People-And-Bears Perrault?"

He turned away, planting his knuckles loudly on the countertop. After a moment, he slumped forward as though thoroughly drained. Almost imperceptibly, Val could see him nod his head.

"Good," she fairly shouted. "Now that you admit you've meddled where you don't belong, let's forget it. You're my guest, and we'll get along—" She broke off. She'd been about to say "fine," but somehow the word seemed hopelessly naive now. Instead, she amended, "We'll get along—*if you keep out of my private business!*"

"Damn!" he whispered through a long sigh. "I'm sorry, Val. Really." As he turned back, his broad shoulders moved with a heaviness she'd never seen before. His expression was melancholy, touchingly so. "Why don't you go on to bed? I think I'll take a look at that dryer."

Surprise clouded Val's features. "But it's so late."

"I couldn't sleep now." Heading toward the mudroom, he murmured, "See you in the morning."

When he'd disappeared, Val leaned against the wall,

feeling peculiarly criminal. Quaid's face had been so stricken when he'd walked away. Damn the man. He thought he was trying to help. For the love of Pete, why couldn't he leave well enough alone? She didn't want his help. She didn't want to dredge up the past, and she certainly didn't intend to confide in Quaid, of all people!

Absently she cleared away the dishes and was about to go to her own bed when she heard a crash from the mudroom. When a muffled groan followed, she didn't even stop to consider what might have happened. She ran, threw open the door and was on her knees beside Quaid's prone body before she realized she'd moved. "Oh, Quaid, are you all right?" Scrambling up next to his chest to inspect the damage, she leaned in between the washer and dryer where Quaid was lying on his back.

He had a small cut on his forehead and was struggling to his elbows.

"What happened," she cried, dabbing at the cut with the clean dish towel she'd carried in with her. "You're bleeding!"

He peered up at her, his gaze narrowed with pain. "I thought you'd gone to bed."

"Thank God, I hadn't! What happened?"

He shook his head to clear his vision and squinted up at her. "I guess when I moved the dryer out I dislodged something from the shelf above."

"Oh, dear." Val scanned the shadows behind the dryer and located the culprit—a brand-new metal container of car wax. She hefted it, flinching at its weight.

"Oh, Quaid, I hope you don't have a concussion. Let me help you sit up."

She slid an arm about his shoulders and eased him into a sitting position against the dryer. Tentatively touching the area, she mused aloud, "It's raising a bump. I'd better get some ice for that."

"I'm okay," he assured her, starting to stand, but she pressed both hands on his shoulders.

"Don't you move. I'll be right back."

Later, with an ice pack on his forehead, she helped him to the couch. He smiled up at her. "I appreciate your concern, but I'm fine. I've come through worse than this."

His blasé remark was meant to make light of his situation, but it only served to remind her of how he'd looked that day she'd airlifted him out of Keystone Canyon. Not knowing what to say, Val dropped to her knees and removed the ice pack. "The lump isn't so bad, but there'll be a bruise."

"What? And mess up my pretty face?" he kidded with a slow grin.

"Egomaniac," Val countered sternly, trying to ignore the thrill that raced up her spine at the sight of his smile.

Their eyes locked, and they found themselves communicating in an unspoken, ancient language. Quaid was telling her that he was fond of her and he'd never intended to hurt her. She, in turn, told him that she knew he hadn't, and she forgave him. There was something quite wonderful about that silent moment they shared, and Val was touched in a way she couldn't explain. Impulsively she smoothed the lock of dark hair that had fallen across his battered brow.

"Val?" Quaid prompted quietly. "Let me help—"

"Don't..." With a sudden, unreasoning need, Val lowered her lips to meet his. "Don't even think," she murmured, speaking more to herself than to him. What madness was this that was driving her to know Quaid in such an intimate way? Other men had tried all kinds of ploys to get her into bed, so why was she sliding up beside Quaid, who was lying there *injured* for heaven's sake? Why was she slipping over him, straddling him, curling her arms wantonly about his neck?

A small sound of pure pleasure escaped her throat as his clever tongue teased her lips and his arms enfolded her within the embrace she'd so foolishly pined for. She could hear the ice pack fall to the floor, and she could feel Quaid's heartbeat quicken in his surprise and delight.

His hands began to explore the curves of her back and hips, and Quaid's guttural groan told her that he was a man possessed with a growing need.

Her woman's core pulsated with desire, and her hips began to move against his thinly clad groin, inspiring wellsprings of pleasure to stir within them both. Feeling his arousal sent Val spiraling even more determinedly toward her objective. Now that she'd unleashed the lusty monster within her, she allowed it to run free.

Lifting her lips from his, she began to trail eager kisses along his jaw. When she came to his flawed chin, she traced the cleft with her tongue, loving the rugged maleness she tasted. "Oh, Quaid," she moaned, "it's been so long—so long...."

Her fingers trembled, fumbling with the sash of his robe, but very quickly she was tracing the mat of hair along his belly with her tongue, nipping and tantalizing, her fervor growing with the urgency of her need. She felt as though she'd been in a deep, dank prison for years and someone had just flung the doors wide, allowing her but a moment to make her escape, to run free in a cool, musky wood.

So sudden and overwhelming was Quaid's sexual

pull that she imagined that she must be going insane. She became frantic to know and see everything she had been so long without—frenzied, crazed in her compulsion to taste, touch, feel, smell everything that was Quaid Perrault. It was as though she must experience him right now, mindlessly, or she never, ever would. She was frightened, but she didn't dare think about why as she trembled with both panic and passion.

Flinging away her turtleneck, she buried her face in the soft mat of hair on his chest, reveling in the feel of his hot, hard body against hers.

After a moment, she become aware that someone very far away was sobbing. She could taste salty tears—and Quaid's hands were no longer questing lovingly across her body. They were holding her quaking shoulders. His voice came to her sounding husky and sad, and he was calling her name.

Lifting her head, she witnessed his heartsick expression, and it sent a shaft of alarm through her, making her shiver with foreboding. "What's wrong?" she whimpered, confused, her nerves ragged. "Don't you want me?"

"Hell, yes, I want you, Val," he murmured, pulling her up to sit within the shelter of his arms. "But, you don't want me—don't want this. Look at you, you're crying, your whole body is shaking. You weren't making love just then, you were trying to rid yourself of a devil." Shrugging off his robe, he laid it across her shoulders. "I don't think having sex with me is the way to do that. Tomorrow you'd just have two devils to deal with."

Humiliated, Val cast him a haunted gaze. She tried to speak, but her lips were numb. Licking them, she tried again. "Quaid..." She wiped away a tear. "I—I don't know what to say." Her broken admission had been so tentative she wasn't sure he could even hear her.

"You don't need to say anything." Standing, he helped her to her feet. "Now, let's get you to bed." Their eyes met and he squeezed her shoulder reassuringly. "Alone."

She was so weak she could hardly stand, so she let him support her weight by leaning heavily on him. "Thank you, Quaid." It came out in a tired, resigned sigh.

"Don't thank me, Val. It's just a thing we men have about making love. We'd rather the lady didn't go into hysterics. It's hard on the ego."

Something in the way he said it, something in the way concern, good humor and genuine affection tangled up in his voice, caused her spirits to lighten fractionally. How he'd managed that so soon after her complete and total humiliation was nothing short of extraordinary.

Her lips quivered in the beginnings of a smile, and she shook her head at herself. What an idiot she was. Feeling somehow cleansed by his caring attitude, she turned her face up to his and smiled feebly. "How can I repay you for your gallantry tonight?"

He smiled back at her. It was a soft expression she knew she would carry in her heart for a long time. Guiding her toward her bedroom door, he suggested, "Just let me be your friend. That's all I'm really up for, anyway."

The remark drew her gaze back to his face. Her expression was skeptical enough to let him know that she wouldn't have believed that five minutes ago.

Unable to disprove her skepticism, he shrugged wryly. "Poor word choice." Dropping his arm from about her, he seemed to be making an effort to further emphasize his desire to move their relationship to a more platonic level.

Silently her mind chided, *What would loving him have been like?*

"Are we friends?" he asked, interrupting her wayward turn of mind. "Or not?"

She turned away to hide a telltale blush, but as she closed the door, she promised, "I'll think about it."

8

EXHILARATING! That was the only way Val could describe her day. She, Quaid and Ross had conquered Nemesis, a particularly difficult ice route. She'd done some front-pointing on icicles so narrow that her crampons had to be planted in a clumsy pigeon-toed position. Maintaining her balance had been almost impossible.

Several times, when she'd been trying to plant her ice tool higher on the glassy surface, she'd found herself swinging wildly away from the shuddering pillar in her effort to get a solid hold. But she'd done it! Right now, she felt as though she could conquer just about any obstacle fate threw her way.

They were a happy threesome on this Valentine's Day as they headed home in Quaid's Jeep to clean up for the Ice Festival welcoming dinner. When they dropped Ross off, he promised to save them two seats at his table, since Val lived farther out of town than he did and—he'd kidded, "Women take so damned long to put on their faces."

Quaid mused that Val kept her face constantly "ready"—a convivial, false face. He hadn't pressed her about anything today. He'd been exactly what she'd wanted him to be, an uninquisitive guest. She'd done well on the climb, and he admired her obstinacy. But there were two sides to that coin, and the perversity that had hoisted her up those frozen falls also kept him at a stiff-armed emotional distance. She smiled, laughed, chattered away about her successful first-time effort at lay-backing icicles on Nemesis. Yet Quaid wasn't buying the bluff that this woman's life was in complete and satisfactory order.

On the drive to her cabin, he faced the fact that trying to help Val tame her inner devil was going to tie him in emotional knots, something he didn't need. Next week at this time, he'd either have climbed Death Scream, died trying, or he'd have chickened out—with disastrous consequences to his already shaken self-worth. He didn't know which would be worse, a fatal fall, or proving himself to be a complete coward.

He must have made a guttural sound—done something telling—for he heard Val shift in her seat as though she'd turned to face him. "Anything wrong?" she asked.

"Not a thing." Val was on his blind side, and he didn't glance her way, keeping his gaze directed on the treacherous stretch of road, but he felt sure she was watching him. He wondered if she'd glimpsed his fear.

THE VALDEZ CIVIC CENTER banquet room was festively decorated with streamers of white and silver. The unique centerpieces at every table were actual crampons, anchoring helium-filled balloons imprinted with the names of Valdez's most notorious frozen waterfalls.

Val was vastly outnumbered by the men among the climbers. Still, there was a smattering of young women; some she recognized, some were new faces. All attending, however, were casually dressed, boisterous, excited and ready for the festival to begin.

"Happy Valentine's Day, Valentine!" shouted two young men in unison, waving and laughing from across the room. Val returned the friendly greeting with an amicable smile and a wave, but inwardly her heart constricted. How ironic, to have a name like Valentine and be so unlovable, unworthy of a man's affections. She hated the holiday and absolutely refused to allow Ross or any of the other men in town to give her anything, insisting she wasn't ready to be anybody's valentine. They assumed it was her grief over John's death, and she allowed them to think that. Only she knew the truth—that she didn't think she could ever be anyone's valentine, ever again.

Once they found Ross, signaling from near the front of the unpretentious room, Val and her houseguest settled in among familiar faces. Except for Quaid and a climber from New Zealand, all the men at Ross's table were local bachelors, delighted to see Val among their number again this year.

Val noticed that Ross had chosen the table where the centerpiece read Death Scream. Though Death Scream had not been officially named yet, Quaid's fall and his haunting cry as he plummeted toward earth, had been witnessed by numerous climbers. Hence, that horrendous ice route had been dubbed Death Scream until someone beat it, and only then would it be officially named by its conqueror.

Val knew why Ross had chosen this table. She knew that it was his pledge to Quaid, that this was the year he'd defeat the killer falls and would have his rightful part in naming it.

She glanced over at Quaid and found that he was staring silently at the balloon as it listed gently in the air—his face unreadable, his gaze narrowed. She wondered what he was thinking.

"Hi, Val."

Feeling a hand on her shoulder, she turned around.

"Oh, hello Andy." Touching his hand affectionately, she asked, "How's the doctoring business?"

He grinned down at her, his wire-rimmed glasses flashing reflected light. "I had a baby this morning. Nine pounds, two ounces."

"Well, I'm happy to see you up and around so quickly," she kidded, playing along with the joke.

As he chuckled at her rejoinder, Andy Embick, expert climber and Valdez general practitioner, spotted Quaid. Val saw Andy's smile fade slightly with concern. When Quaid noticed the doctor looking at him, he nodded.

Andy returned the nod and offered, "Glad to see you back, Perrault."

Quaid's contemplative expression had vanished and he was smiling at the veteran climber. "Thanks, Andy. Good to be back."

"You heard that Ben LeRoy cratered last year when he was free-soloing on Wowie Zowie."

Quaid frowned, shaking his head. "No. He okay?"

Andy shrugged. "Broke his tibia, smashed his jaw. He recovered, all right, but he's had an acute change of heart about climbing ice. Sold all his equipment. I hear he's into golf, now."

"I can see his point," Quaid admitted frankly.

Andy's laugh was a little melancholy. "I'm sure you can. Well, good luck this year."

"You, too," Quaid offered easily.

Patting Val's shoulder again, Andy began to edge away. "I'd better join my party. See you on the ice."

Val smiled at him, calling, "Break a leg, Doc."

"Very droll," he shouted back. "I'll remember that the next time you need a miracle cure from me!"

Laughing delightedly, Val missed the fact that

Quaid had turned away to stare at nothing in particular, his jaw muscles bunching in agitation.

Dinner consisted of the now-traditional Carboloading Spaghetti Feast, topped off by Baked Alaska. Quaid found himself hardly tasting the food, and paying scant attention as the president of the Valdez Alpine Club made his welcoming remarks. He'd heard it all before.

Trying to forget his fear, he passed the time by watching the men at his table. They preened and postured like peacocks for Val's benefit. Yet Val, aware of her companions' intentions, was totally unresponsive, pretending not to notice the mating ritual. People from other tables, drawn by the laughter and brash commentary of exploits on the ice, were turning to find out who was so damnably enticing at the Death Scream table.

It wasn't difficult to tell, once they spied Val, the solitary woman, dressed in an emerald-green knit turtleneck, her blond-brown hair drifting about her shoulders in thick, frolicsome tendrils crying out to be tamed, stroked....

Quaid clamped his jaws tightly. She looked fine, he amended circumspectly—clean and neat in her green sweater and slacks—actually, she was very lovely. It was a reluctant admission, but it was the truth. He didn't blame the men at all. If he was in the market for a lover, Val would top the list.

She laughed, and the sound touched off something deep in his gut. Shifting so that he could furtively adjust his jeans, he took a sip of his coffee, taking great pains to notice the taste. Strong, black and lukewarm, the liquid was in no way a tempting substitute for Val's kiss— "So, Val," a redhead called from across the circular table, short-circuiting Quaid's train of thought. "You gonna climb Killer Death Fang Falls?"

Her gay laughter drifted over him again, and Quaid shifted once more, cursing against the rim of his cup. He needed to be affected by her like he needed ice flaking off in his eye!

"No. It's only Grade Three. First thing Monday, though, we're doing Broken Dreams."

"A Grade Six? Hell, Val, that's a grim climb. You've really improved since last year. Maybe I'll try it Tuesday."

She grinned at him. "You've improved, too, then, Clyde."

He shrugged diffidently. "Who're you climbing with?"

She indicated Ross, who was to her immediate left, and Quaid, who'd had to sit several chairs away. "These guys. They've been giving me private lessons."

Quaid felt several envious pairs of eyes on him, and he grinned amiably even though he didn't feel like it. Hell! They all acted as though they were in a competition for her and Quaid was some kind of interloper. If they only knew how little either he or Val wanted a relationship with each other, they'd breathe easy.

"Hey, aren't you the guy who cratered—?"

Quaid heard Val's tiny gasp, but he didn't look in her direction. Instead he faced the speaker, a brawny transplanted Californian by the name of Leon. Lowering his coffee cup to the table, he remarked quietly, "Four years ago."

"And you're back?" Leon whistled low and long. "Did you figure out what you did wrong? You know what they say, there are no accidents in ice climbing, only—"

"I know," Quaid interjected quietly, "only mistakes in judgment."

"Yeah. You aren't going to try Death Scream again, are you?"

"Friday."

"The hell you say! Free-soloing?"

Quaid shook his head. "No. It's a fierce route. I used a back rope last time. It failed me. This time I'm not going alone."

"Oh? Kind of a step down—I mean, having to share the glory. Wouldn't you say?"

Quaid's only response to the pride-lacerating remark was to take a long, slow sip of his coffee, but his narrowed, incredulous gaze remained trained on Leon, who, Val noticed, was beginning to squirm under its piercing heat.

"Who's going with you?" Clyde asked, filling the breach of awkward silence.

"Ross and I are," Val blurted, finally finding her voice after her shock at Leon's verbal slap.

Every head at the table jerked to stare at her. "Sure you are, Val." Clyde laughed. "You and the angel Gabriel."

Everyone laughed except Quaid, Ross and Val. Quaid knew why neither he nor Ross was laughing. Val was hell-bent to try it. Quaid noticed that Ross was looking at her with foreboding in his eyes, but he said nothing.

When the chuckling had died down, Val opened her mouth to protest, but Quaid interjected, "I'd thought you'd like to try Broken Dreams on Friday, Val. I'm sure one or two of these men would be happy to accompany you while Ross and I—"

"No, thanks," Val threw in quickly and definitely.

"I've been wanting to climb Death Scream for quite a while, and today I decided I was ready to do it."

Ross swallowed visibly, his face going gray. "Val, honey, are you sure this is what you want to do?"

She squeezed his hand. "You've been a great teacher, Ross. I know I can."

"Like hell you can," Quaid cut in, his fear revving into high gear. "You're not going up Death Scream next Friday, Val, and that's that."

She turned to grace him with an unblinking stare. The only evidence that she was perturbed was the tightening of her fingers over Ross's hand. "What?" she asked very calmly. Though her expression remained pleasant, her eyes snapped a less placid message.

"You heard me. No way are you going to climb that hellish ice. No *damned* way. Do I make myself clear?" He could feel sweat bead on his forehead, his anxiety was so strong.

Val rose slowly, majestically from her chair, her chin lifted to such an imperial angle that Quaid had the feeling she might exclaim, "Off with his head!"

Instead she smiled frostily, her controlled facade in place, and informed him, "You can't tell me what to do, Quaid. I plan to make that climb with you and Ross, and any attempt to stop me will be nothing short of criminal."

The hush that had fallen over their table was palpable. Quaid stared at her in utter disbelief. She couldn't mean this. How in the hell could he keep his concentration honed in on his own survival with her tagging along, thinking—in her vast and naive innocence—that she was equipped for such a climb?

His voice so thick it was almost inaudible, he countered, "It would be criminal for me to allow you to go."

Her blue eyes flashed stubborn fire. "Don't dictate to me. You have no right."

With that, she spun away and walked out of the hall.

Quaid scanned the faces around the table. Every pair of eyes was trained on him, every expression ominous. After the moment had dragged on for much too long, Quaid demanded wearily, "I realize that none of you have tried to climb Death Scream, but you must realize Val isn't ready to attempt it. Why didn't any of you tell her how crazy her idea was?"

Ross, his pallor still evident, leaned across the table and scowled at Quaid. "Because, you ass, when you've been around her as long as we have, you'll find out that *nobody* tells Valentine Larrabee what to do. She's her own woman. She's strong, and she doesn't take that macho crap off anybody. There's not a damned thing any one of us—including *you*—can do about it if she decides to climb Death Scream."

"Like hell!" Quaid growled. "Val is a lot of great things, but she's not as in control as you think." Pushing up from his chair, he ground out disgustedly, "You people are blinder than I am if you can't see that."

BY THE TIME VAL REACHED the bottom of the civic center steps, she had to lean against the side of the building to keep from sagging to her knees. She was shaking badly from her attempt to appear unruffled. For a long moment she breathed deeply, watching each agitated breath crystallize in the night air.

Quaid could read people better than most, and she knew he could tell she had problems. But she didn't plan to put up with his constant interference, no matter how well meant. "No, by heaven!" she swore under her breath. She wouldn't allow him to trespass on her personal life—let alone become part of it!

How dare he treat her as though he owned her! She'd fought so hard, shown such toughness to cover her inadequacy all these years. Then he'd ambled into town and, with a look, a kiss, a touch, had begun to crack her well-fortified barriers. She didn't dare allow him to do that, and if throwing their relationship into a fierce competition would put him off, then so be it. Something drastic had to be done.

Clasping her hands and then unclasping them, she finally stuck them into her coat pockets. It was done now. She'd announced her plan in public, so there was no backing out. Quaid may not like it, but he was a big boy. He'd just have to deal with it.

Climbing Death Scream would serve a double purpose: keep Quaid on an equal, competitive level, and prove herself worthwhile—or at least worthy in some sector of her life though, admittedly, not in the area of human relationships.

She realized now that she'd subconsciously decided long ago that Death Scream would be her test. She had to pass it to prove something to herself, for herself. Climbing Death Scream could give her a much needed victory in her life—a shot at control. Big failures required big successes! The fact that the climb would now be doing double duty was just fine with her.

Let Quaid suffer a little for a change. Besides, there was no real danger. They'd have ropes and ice screws. They might not make it all the way to the top, but they wouldn't die. Quaid's mistake last time was trying it solo and with simply a back rope—something attempted only by expert climbers and in the best conditions.

Quaid had been there once—at the top of the heap. Apparently this time he wasn't interested in retaining his position among die-hard Alpinists. He just wanted to complete the climb up Death Scream and erase its nickname, no doubt a painful one from him. It was an ego-oriented return, granted, but an understandable one. Well, with ropes, belays, protection and partners, he'd do it. *Darn him!* Why did he have to get so hot under the collar about it?

QUAID WATCHED HER from behind the door he was holding ajar. Her expression was sad and hardened with determination. Behind him, down the hall from the entrance lobby, he could hear a burst of laughter as a slide presentation of last year's festival began.

Quaid was reluctant to follow Val, knowing she wanted to be alone. But he was loath to leave her out there in the unforgiving chill. After a few grudging minutes, he shrugged on his parka. It was just Val's pride that had taken over. Having made her presumptuous statement in front of witnesses, she simply couldn't admit she was wrong to their faces. She'd come to realize the folly of her remark long before Friday rolled around. She probably already had.

He smiled halfheartedly, having convinced himself that she'd admit her mistake soon enough. For a minute she'd made him feel threatened and apprehensive. He didn't need the complication she'd thrown at him. It had been a lousy shock—like being batted in the back of the head by a testy bear. But now that she'd had a chance to cool off, he knew she'd have to admit she'd been hotheaded and premature.

Presuming the best, he pushed open the door, drawing her glittering gaze. Her distracted expression grew even darker, and Quaid approached with appropriate caution.

His long-legged gait, so familiar to Val, inspired an unwelcome rush of desire, and she uttered a soundless blasphemy. How could her body betray her so? Disillusioned with herself, she dragged her eyes from his approaching form to watch a shooting star streak through the black eternity of space and disappear.

"Make a wish?" came his deep voice.

"You wouldn't want to know."

She could tell he was very near her now, but she refused to face him, her ire was so near the boiling point, she didn't dare. She might be forced to slap his arrogant face. Flinching inwardly, she immediately regretted the thought. That wounded countenance had suffered enough damage as it was.

Contrite over her hostile turn of mind, her anger at him ebbed—if just a bit. With misgivings, she faced him and was struck again by the beauty etched on those splendid, marred features. The streetlight that towered a few feet away served as an artist's brush to embellish the ruggedness of his jaw and the wide, angular thrust of his cheekbones. The scar that ran across the cleft in his chin glistened like a meandering stream bisecting a lusty landscape. She felt an aberrant need to trace a finger along that absorbing flaw.

"Are you ready to go home?" he asked, breaking into her thoughts.

Crossing her arms before her, she tried not to be affected by his nearness. Her response was defensively curt, "Oh? You're allowing me to make my own decision? What a quaint idea."

He looked appropriately chastened. Taking her arm, he steered her toward his Jeep. "I assume that's a yes."

"You're a man of many assumptions, Mr. Perrault," she charged, her voice controlled, but just barely.

Refusing to be baited, he said no more until they were both settled in his four-wheeler and headed out of town. "The dinner was good, don't you think?" he remarked, hoping the subject would be inoffensive.

Instead of the innocuous response he expected, Val lurched around toward him in her bucket seat, slamming a hand down on the dash. "What exactly is your problem, Quaid? Afraid a woman can succeed at something that almost killed you?"

It had been a spiteful thing to say, and she could see the results of her cruelty in the fierce line that formed where his pleasantly upturned lips had been an instant before. She blanched at her handiwork, but knew that she had to make their rift deep and unbreachable. If she'd ever acted tough in her life, she had to do so now. She had to make him angry, competitive. They would spend their passions on ice sheets rather than between bed sheets. It would be better for them both in the long run, she promised herself. But seeing his profile, so hurt yet filled with potent manliness, she was hard-pressed to continue.

Forcing herself, she challenged, "Why are you so afraid to have me go along? Is it your raging ego? Would it kill you to have a woman accomplish the climb alongside you? You'll notice Ross didn't go up in flames about it, and neither did the other climbers at the table." On her knees now, she edged closer to his stiffened form. "Is it pure conceit that drives you, or is it something else? What exactly is *your* problem?"

A brutal harshness had formed around his mouth, a grim solidness she had never seen before. But she imagined a number of vanquished CEOs had known the look quite intimately. Very quietly he cautioned, "Don't turn this into a damned contest, Val."

Feeling terribly threatened by Quaid's invasions— both physical and emotional—she was damned well going to put a quick and deadly end to it. She was going to assert herself as she'd never done before. Maybe she was overreacting, maybe she was being insensitive and contemptible, yet even in the face of his distress, she fought the tenderness that threatened her resolve. She was set on doing this climb, and neither Quaid Perrault nor God himself, was going to stop her!

She stared at his hard profile, wondering vaguely if he might fling out an arm and backhand her into the window. He looked that angry. But there was something else in his stony silhouette, something in the way a muscle tugged beneath the patch that swathed his ruined eye—something like dismay. Was Quaid carrying around a dark secret, too? Was it more than just ego?

She watched him sitting there, rigid and silent, for a long time before she ventured, "What are you really trying to accomplish by climbing Death Scream, Quaid?"

He swung into her parking area. The Jeep's tires crunched loudly on the crust of packed snow as he slowed to a stop. Switching off the key, he turned to face her. His expression was drawn and haggard. "Dammit, Val. Don't do this." He held up a clenched fist. "It takes concentration—concentration like you wouldn't believe. You can't let up for a second."

Drumming his fist on the steering wheel, he paused for an ominous minute before he went on. "Death Scream is a thousand-foot bundle of sword-thin ice pillars. The delicacy needed to plant an ice tool is unbelievable. It's the same for ice screws. Protection is almost nonexistent. An ice screw pulls out under the load of a single carabiner, so the chance of stopping to rest is almost nil. With you along it'll take us one and a half times as long to climb the route. Are you strong enough for that? I doubt it. Most likely you'll get too tired, flame out, and force us to quit.

"Even if you don't tire, in a fraction of a second you could shear off and fall. *You could die,* Val. Don't underestimate Death Scream. Believe me, I..." He paused, frowned and turned away. "And as for being beside me—don't make me laugh. Only one person can be at the sharp end of the rope. Only one person has that honor—and that risk. You'll be nothing up there but a liability. If either Ross or I take a long fall, we'll cause a huge jerk on the rope. You're small. You couldn't grip it tightly enough to hold the strain. The ice is too thin, the anchors are poor. You might crater with us, if they pull. Don't you see that?" Without waiting for an answer, he yanked open his door and stepped out.

With angry strides he came around to her side of the Jeep. She jumped down and braved his animosity. "I won't be a liability!"

"Like hell!"

"I won't! You'll see!"

"Then climb the damn thing solo. Do it tomorrow." His voice had grown as cold as death.

She swallowed several times but managed to face his lethal gaze. "You know I can't do that." Her admission came out in a mumbled whisper.

"I know...." His powerful shoulders sagged noticeably, his gaze glittering with some unutterable emotion. His disconcerting perusal unsettled Val. Despair engulfing her, she blurted, "You told me once you owed me. Well, now I'm calling in the debt. Take me with you, Quaid. You owe me this chance." Balling her hands, she held her breath for his reply.

He focused on the small, acrimonious gesture. Flat voiced, he said, "I won't pay you back for helping save my life by putting yours in danger."

She groaned in exasperation. "That's a cop-out if I ever heard one."

"Val. I have to make this climb, and I can't afford—" He cut himself off, his expression registering self-disgust. Clearly he hadn't intended to say so much. Without waiting for her to ask the obvious question, he pivoted away and tramped off toward the cabin.

"Can't afford what?" Val asked in a whisper, but not until long after he'd gone inside. The wind was picking up, and she could feel a flurry of snowflakes tease her nose, her cheeks, her chin. She looked around, registering where she was. Without much interest, she squinted up at the sky. The moon was obscured now, and only the lights from the cabin windows illuminated little bands of night.

Flakes twinkled as they danced through the yellow glow from her kitchen window. It was really starting to come down, and the night had the heavy feel of a storm that would last until dawn. But with an average wintertime accumulation of three hundred inches, snow wasn't particularly worthy of a news bulletin in Valdez. Hunching down in her coat, she struck out for the cabin, unconsciously treading in Quaid's footsteps.

9

QUAID LAY AWAKE, his fingers laced behind his head as he stared at the ceiling. Undulating shadows of a fitful fire illuminated the beams over the living area. The squeak-squeak of Val's aging rocking chair came at rapid intervals, a telling message that she was angry beyond words.

Val had been rocking for a solid hour, and the quick squeak-squeak, squeak-squeak, squeak-squeak had not diminished its overwrought pace for even a minute. She was nursing a seething fury that wasn't winding down.

Squeak-squeak, squeak-squeak, squeak-squeak...

Quaid closed his eyes, only to find that his head was beginning to pound. No medieval torture chamber could have exerted more pain on him than the continuous squeaking of Val's rocking chair. His only consolation was that she probably didn't know how her simmering anger was punishing him—small comfort though that was.

He could picture her down there, wrapped in an afghan, one fuzzy slipper tucked beneath her, while Billy Bob lolled on the couch, the dog's questioning eyes on her restive mistress.

Opening his eyes, he focused on the shadows snaking across the ceiling. He had to admit Val had a point—though a minute one. His reaction to her pronouncement that she was going to climb Death Scream must have seemed Neanderthal with his I-am-man-therefore-man-must-protect-woman harangue. It was as outdated as saying, "The little woman belongs in the kitchen."

Still, he'd rather be thought of as a Neanderthal than a coward. And no power on earth could have dragged the truth from him—that he was gut-wrenching scared. His confidence in himself was zero. When he'd fallen before, he'd lost much of his self-worth as a man, and he didn't know what there might be left to salvage—if anything.

He could have told her all that, but the idea of laying too much out in the open made him feel sick inside. He'd learned long ago to internalize his feelings. His father had spent Quaid's formative years terrorizing and abusing him to the point where Quaid had learned that if he was going to get any help in this world, it would have to be from his own two hands.

Quaid's actions might have appeared ruthless and unfeeling when he'd been amassing his fortune. Because of his upbringing, he'd never had the luxury of discussing his problems, so as an adult he never explained himself or made excuses. He just took what life dished out and then silently, and with an iron will, clawed his way over obstacles. It was true that he'd changed his life-style and had put his grasping existence behind him, but that didn't change thirty-six years of keeping his problems to himself and solving them by himself.

There was no damned way he was going to tell a living soul that he felt empty—unworthy of calling himself a man. A week ago, he'd finally been able to admit it aloud to God and to the damned ice fall in Keystone Canyon, but that was as far as he could go. Val would just have to continue thinking whatever she wanted to think about him, because she was *not* going to hear the truth from him.

His fear gnawed at him, and he felt himself break out in a cold sweat as he relived the danger involved in climbing Death Scream. There would be times when the ice would be so rotten and riddled with air pockets that he'd be unable to get his ice tools to stick effectively. After hours on the vertical ice, in his utter fatigue, he could chop through his own lifeline—or Val could. She might freak out and go into hysterics five hundred feet up. He'd seen it happen to men with more experience than she had. Even *he* could freak, considering his state of mind.

And there was always the chance that some skimpy pillar he'd be forced to scale might break away and plummet earthward, carrying him to his death. Who was to say he wouldn't drag both Ross and Val with him? Over and above wanting the damned glory, and not having to depend on the questionable performance of others, he'd opted to go solo the first time so that he couldn't endanger anyone else's life. Even though his primary motivation for going solo had been selfish, he was thankful he'd made that decision then.

The last time he'd climbed Death Scream, he'd been at the top of the heap, "the hardest of the hard men," in ice-climbers vernacular, and he'd lost it—his concentration, his strength and nearly his life. Now he had to continuously fight to keep from visibly trembling whenever Death Scream came into his line of sight. With so little nerve, how did he dare allow Val to follow him up? It would be like the blind leading the...

His lips quivered in an ironic smile at the appropriate figure of speech. To conquer Death Scream, he had to have perfect mental focus, Herculean strength, and though his adrenaline would be pumping furiously, his nerves had to be as calm as a sleeping baby's. With everything else he had to think about, Val would divert his attention whether she planned to or not, and he resented that. Resented her for putting him in the position to have to worry about her.

What was it that drove her to think about trying such a foolish stunt? Was it the same devil that Ross had referred to as grief over her husband's death? He still didn't swallow that story. Val's troubles went deeper than that—no matter how much she'd loved the guy.

Squeak-squeak, squeak-squeak, squeak-squeak—

"Dammit to hell!" he ground out under his breath. Throwing his legs over the side of the bed, he made quick work of the stairs. He reached the bottom of the steps and moved to face her, clad only in his sweatpants, his stance wide and combative, his hands clenched.

The dusky half-light of the lapping fire made her look fragile yet terribly stern. He felt a stab of regret at what he had to say.

Val's rocker came to a halt, and she lifted a cold gaze to clash with his, her expression a mixture of fear and contempt.

"Hell, Val," he began, his tone biting, "what is it about your husband's death that's making you overreact this way? Is your need to climb Death Scream some sort of crazy death wish?"

Val stared at him, mute with horror. She felt the blood drain from her face, and her body went stiff. Too shocked to do anything but sit there, she could only clutch the arms of her rocker with white-knuckled fists. "How did…" She began in a trembly whisper, her alarm slowly being replaced with confusion. "How did you know this has anything to do with John?"

His anger receded into astonishment. It had been a

wild off-the-wall guess—a needling suspicion hovering around the edges of his mind. "I didn't," he answered, his voice low in the stark quiet. "Until now…"

She looked unsure and frightened as he watched anguish swim in her eyes, then tears spill unchecked down her cheeks. With a welling up of compassion, he knelt beside her chair and engulfed her hand in the warmth of his, squeezing it. "Tell me, Val," he spoke carefully, choosing his words deliberately. "What happened between you and John that scarred you so badly that you have to risk your life to redeem yourself?"

He could feel the pent-up tension in her body as she turned away from his probing stare. "Don't ask me that," she begged, her voice broken and small.

"I have to," he told her honestly. "I don't want to resent you, Val. And I will if you insist on climbing Death Scream."

She visibly retreated from him, seeming to shrink in size, as well as spirit. Suddenly her mask was gone, and she was no one he'd ever seen before. She was quaking and terrified, not the dauntless Valentine he'd come to know. Her profile became fixed with some terrible emotion as she yanked from his touch, vaulting out of the chair. Throwing off her afghan, she darted away from him.

Val felt her chest constrict, and her breathing came hard and painfully. The word "resent" had brought everything back—her fear of being resented and then rejected by someone just as she'd resented and rejected John for his weakness. Horrified that Quaid might gouge her ugly secret from her, she rushed away from him blindly, fleeing from the man who had hit so close to the truth.

Before her mind had cleared enough to evaluate her actions, she ran outside into the swirling maelstrom and had the 4×4's engine straining to its mechanical limits, gunning it to life in the sub-zero temperature. She had no idea where the keys had come from, but right now, she didn't care.

Backing wildly around, she skidded toward the front porch. When she spun the wheel to maneuver the four-wheeler toward the road, she caught sight of Quaid in the headlights. His bare chest, an impressive contoured frieze, was captured within the stark lights for the split second it took to propel the vehicle away from the cabin.

Trying to wipe away the vision, she stomped impatiently on the gas pedal. All she wanted in life was to escape his persistent inquisition. Fishtailing along the narrow road, she lost control and slid sideways. With a scream of panic, she fought to straighten the Jeep, but to no avail.

Diving for safety, she felt the impact with the twelve-foot snowdrift along the roadside, and her body slid until she was sitting upright on the driver's-side window, her head resting in the recess where the passenger's seat cushion joined the backrest.

After a breathless moment assessing damage to her body, Val breathed a ragged sigh. She felt no pain anywhere, except for a slow throbbing where her thigh had landed against the door latch. Looking around, she felt disoriented in the overturned machine. The passenger door loomed above her head, and the windshield was half-buried in snow.

"Oh, Lord," she cried. "What have I done to Quaid's Jeep?"

Reality having fully set in, she was ashamed of herself; where did she think she'd been going? What good had driving off in a raging snowstorm done—especially considering she'd managed to get only about thirty yards from the cabin?

A thud on the hood attracted her attention, and she shot a frightened gaze upward, startled to see Quaid peering in the upper half of the windshield. "Are you hurt?" he shouted over the roar of the wind.

Val noticed he was still bare chested, but he'd thrown on his parka, though he hadn't taken the time to zip it.

She scrambled up on her knees and then just as quickly tumbled against the upright portion of the driver's seat. She guessed that the Jeep must be tilted so that only the passenger door and front right wheel were exposed above the snow. It must have skidded around until its rear end had slid off into the ditch. Lying on her back, she shouted, "Go home, Quaid." She waved him off weakly. "You'll catch your death out there. Just leave me—"

Apparently he had no plans to obey her or even wait to hear her whole speech. The passenger door sluggishly began to creak open as he fought gravity and a snow-clogged wind to force it up far enough for him to slip inside.

Once he'd joined her, he had to lie across the back portion of both front seats in a semi-crouched position. Val found herself thrust into the unsettling proximity of his snow-spangled hips as gravity forced him to straddle her. Now her humiliation turned into fiery embarrassment mixed with an annoying rebirth of sexual frustration.

"Oh, Quaid," she moaned just above a whisper. "Go away."

"Are you hurt?" he demanded again, his fright making him sound angry.

"Can't you just go away? What does it take for you

to leave someone be—a cocked shotgun?'' She shook her head. ''For an intuitive man, you're pretty dense at times.''

He moved quickly, grasping her arms and pulling her upright until she was stretched beneath him, her face a scant inch below his. ''What does it take for you to reach out to a friend, dammit,'' he grumbled. ''A slab at the morgue?'' With his anger now equaling hers, he charged, ''You damn near killed yourself just now. You realize that, don't you?''

''Oh, don't be so melodramatic!'' she countered, working to hide her mortification.

''Me? Melodramatic? I'm not the one who made scrap metal out of my Jeep.''

His words hit her hard. Crestfallen and shamed, her eyes became awash with tears as his remark ripped away the remnants of her bravado. Finally without defense, she cried, ''Oh, Quaid…I'm so…sorry about your car.'' She bit her lip to still its trembling. ''I'll pay for it, of course.''

His curse was brief and succinct. ''You can't even afford to get your VW out of hock,'' he reminded her with devastating frankness. ''Forget my Jeep. I've got other cars. You, lady, have got more immediate problems.''

The vehemence of his voice sent shivers up her spine as he added, ''I'm not letting you out of this wreck until you tell me what the hell is with you. You'll never heal if you don't face your devil and deal with it.'' He didn't add that that was exactly the reason he was back in Valdez. Maybe if he could get her to admit her own fears, she wouldn't have to carry through on her crazy vow to climb with him.

''I won't tell you, Quaid!'' she heard herself cry out.

"Yes, you will," he promised, his voice oddly quiet, even encouraging. "You must."

Val wished she hadn't so recklessly taken his car. Now, not only were they without transportation, but she was in exactly the position she'd fought so long and hard to avoid—body to body with Quaid Perrault. His bare chest was pressed against the cotton knit of her nightshirt. Unfortunately, in their haste, neither of them had taken the time to fasten their parkas.

She swallowed, staring up into his arresting, ravaged face. Melting snow sparkled on his cheeks and lashes—and mouth. His apprehensive expression had dissolved into one of reassurance, and those glistening lips lifted in a comforting half smile. "Let me be your friend, Valentine."

There was something carnal in the tone of his voice, something she didn't think Quaid had meant to declare, but she'd heard it. Plainly, so had he, for she saw him wince. Immediately he tried to lift himself slightly away.

"Damn gear shift," he muttered, and Val realized he could retreat only so far.

"It's okay, Quaid," she assured him, lying flagrantly. This all too intimate confrontation was far from okay. She didn't like being quite so aware of a man—it went against her life plan of steering clear of entanglements. "Let's just go back to the cabin."

"No," he protested in a whisper that held a dusky warning.

"No?" Her eyes grew round with frightened anticipation.

"I told you you weren't going anywhere until you told me what you were trying to run away from."

Icy snow rat-a-tatted as though a machine gun were strafing the windshield. It was a bleak, restless night, matching Val's raw emotions. She cut her gaze away to stare down at the steering wheel behind Quaid's massive calves. When her eyes followed his legs down, she was aghast to see that he was barefoot. With a sharp intake of breath, she shot her gaze back up at his face, protesting, "Quaid, your feet! Haven't you ever heard of frostbite? We've got to go back—"

She'd begun to scramble out from under him, reaching upward toward the door handle, but he grabbed her hands. "I've climbed ice for a lot of years, Val. My hands and feet are accustomed to extreme cold. Don't change the subject. You've reached your day of reckoning. It's here and it's now, whether you like it or not." His gaze shimmered with promise, and she shuddered with the knowledge that he meant every word he'd said—quietly, yet with the hard edge of a man accustomed to dealing in ironclad contracts. She knew instinctively that he would brook no further objections.

Without warning, the safe little world she'd built for herself cracked and fell to pieces, crumbling about her as it had during the earthquake of 1964. Her house had teetered crazily and then just disintegrated, and she'd been thrown to her knees in the rubble. Helpless, she'd watched in terror as her parents had plunged through a crack in the world to be crushed by falling debris. She'd been left with nothing, alone, a defenseless little girl.

Now she felt the very same way emotionally—powerless, lying amid the rubble of her guilt. The stress of the years of hiding her failing, Quaid's unrelenting probing, this foolish accident and tonight's bone-rattling cold—it was finally just too much to bear—like a major earthquake in her soul.

Involuntarily her body began to shake, and unknowingly her fingers squeezed his tightly. "Oh, Quaid," she whimpered. "You'll hate me...."

"Try me," he whispered near her ear, his encompassing body a haven in the frigid, turbulent night.

She would have sunk dejectedly to her knees but for his weight against her. Trying to control the revulsion in her voice, she began through a disheartened groan, "John was ill for a long time. An operation would have given him a fifty-fifty chance to live a normal life, but he was afraid to risk it. You see, he had the same chance of dying on the operating table. So he chose to merely exist, and for the four years he did manage to survive, but he retreated into fear.

"He shut me out, shut out my love, shut out any chance for a normal married life with me." As she told her story, she refused to look at Quaid's face. But she was aware that he continued to hold her hands.

"I—I grew to despise John for his cowardice."

With her eyes cast downward, she missed Quaid's distress at her word "cowardice." What would she think of him, Quaid wondered, if she knew—

"I grew to resent him horribly!" Val cried unaware of her companion's thoughts. She only knew she hated hearing her confession out loud. The words came bitter and harsh to her tongue, but once begun, it was as though a dam had burst in her heart, and every pent-up, miserable drop, no matter how stagnant and putrid, had to pour out. "I was the worst kind of selfish, base person to turn away from my husband, a man I cared for more than I cared for my own life. But in those terrible four years, I watched my love for him shrivel and die and turn into contempt and resentment."

Her voice broke and she choked back a sob. As if reliving a nightmare, she shook her head and squeezed her eyes shut. It took her a moment to control her voice enough to continue. "He died in my arms, Quaid, and it was my fault that he did. If I hadn't been so selfish—insisted that we go out on our anniversary—he might have lived another month, another year—" Her voice broke. "Don't you see—I've got to be strong—got to prove myself. I can't lean on anyone—never love anyone—because, someday that someone could resent me, think of me as a burden. I couldn't take that. I don't know how John did...." Her chin began to quiver as fresh tears spilled from between her closed lids.

For a long, tangible moment she could hear nothing but the howling, battering wind. All she could feel was the length of Quaid's body and the heavy thudding of his heart against her breasts. She could smell the coffee warmth of his breath and a hint of musky after-shave. When the silence had become suffocating, she forced herself to look into his face, to confront the loathing she would see there.

He was watching her closely, narrowly, but his expression held no malice, no disgust. His gaze gleamed with moisture, and she was stunned. The possibility of such a phenomenon occurring had never entered her mind. Quaid Perrault was close to tears.

"Val, you may not realize it yet," he began, his voice hoarse yet admiring, "but the healing has begun."

She allowed her lids to loll shut and wearily shook her head, her hair a tangle around her face. "Just because I told you my nasty secret, it doesn't mean anything has changed...."

"You're wrong, Val. You've faced it—said it out loud. It's damned hard to do, but it's a beginning."

With a short, miserable laugh she asked, "What would you know about human weakness—a man like you? You're strong. Defeat isn't in your nature. Look at you," she cried, her voice a tattered whisper. "How many men would come back to climb Death Scream after they'd almost died?"

Mortified, she pushed at his chest, wanting to get away, wishing she'd never told this man, who couldn't possibly understand cowardliness, about her terrible flaw. She whimpered, "You have no more idea of what it would take to rid me of my shame than you know how to—how to *fly!*"

A flash of pain darkened his expression before he admitted, "You're right about one thing. I proved I couldn't fly four years ago, didn't I."

Seeing his sadness, hearing the tremendous regret in his voice, she was thrown off balance. She'd been so intent on her defense, she'd forgotten that, though he was recovered now, he'd had to fight a terrible battle to get back to where he was today. She'd given him no credit for that, and of course, that was what he had been trying to tell her. Healing begins with the first painful step. His had been physical—hers was emotional.

Unsure of what to say or do, she found herself staring at his shadowed features. After a moment, a vague half smile flickered across his lips, drawing her gaze to his lips. "Feeling better?" he queried softly.

"I—well—"

"Good."

The uplifted corner of his mouth boded nothing sinister or sarcastic, but was soft, yet in some unnameable way, dangerous. She took a deep breath, trying to control her awareness of the gentle, sexy expression, a problem made acute since she was pressed fully against him.

Intuition told her that now would be a good time to suggest that they leave, but words failed her. Quaid brushed a stray wisp of hair from her distracted face, his breath warm on her lips.

It was taking all her waning effort to fight off the hypnotic effect he had on her. Feeling wooden and hesitant, she pressed herself as far back in the seat cushions as possible. "Quaid?" she whispered, her voice hushed, almost as though in prayer.

"Hmm?"

"You're not…"

As his lips met hers, he murmured, "Dammed if I'm not…"

She was so beautiful, so courageous and so tortured. He was confused about why he was kissing her, why he had to drag her into his arms and know, again, the reluctant invitation of her mouth. He only knew that he wanted to comfort her, to make her feel cared for. No, it was more than that. He wanted to thrill her, make her cry out with joy and passionate release. He wanted to make love to the woman. And he knew that once he did, he wouldn't be able to saunter happily away, whistling nonchalantly over an enjoyable one-night stand. He'd be emotionally involved with her, and dammit, that was exactly what he *didn't* need right now.

Even as his mind counted off the reasons that this seduction was the most foolhardy thing he'd ever done, his lips were devouring hers, his tongue dipping, taunting, exciting.

He heard her soft moan, felt her hands come up beneath his parka to cling to his back. Her hips pressed familiarly against his groin, igniting him with a need to become a pulsing part of her, to know her deeply, to become one with her sweet, sad soul.…

Their kisses deepened and became electric, sparking and arcing in the confined space. Val burned and sizzled, her body becoming charged with a revitalized zest for life. She'd forgotten how quickening the touch of a man could be, and she rejoiced in the torrid rebirth of that knowledge.

Mad with pleasure, she fumbled with the lacing of his sweatpants, her kisses growing urgent along his jaw. She sighed as she finally loosened the cords enough to dip her fingers inside.

Quaid groaned at her delicate yet charged touch, and he found her mouth once again, his teeth nipping, teasing, his tongue searching, inciting her to greater and greater levels of excitement as she satisfied herself that he was a man ready to lift her toward ecstasy.

She held him, reveling in the total intimacy, the womanly power she possessed.

"Val..." he rasped against her throat, his kisses trailing to the scooped neck of her nightshirt. His hands too were busy, dragging up the tail of her gown, his fingers trailing icy fire along her rib cage and slowly, tantalizingly, moving to cup her breasts.

She arched toward him, pressing her feminine softness into his large, knowing hands. Too long celibate, too long rejected by the man she'd loved, her body raged with a wild, unstoppable need to be touched, held and brought soaring through the gates of paradise.

She shouldn't allow this crazy thing to go on, for Quaid to slip his searching fingers beneath the scant barrier of her panties, but she sighed tremulously as he did, her own fingers stroking more boldly in their loving exploration.

He groaned, lowering his lips to press a kiss between her breasts. With his breath coming in short harsh gasps, he murmured unevenly, "Are you sure you want to do this here?"

She was insane with passionate need, and it took her a moment to realize he'd spoken at all. She stared at him, her vision blurry with the tears of her heightened emotion.

Though she opened her mouth to speak, no words came, her throat was so choked with desire. Trying again, she whispered, "Don't you?" It came out anxiously, as though she were afraid he'd had second thoughts.

He graced her with a heart-stopping grin, kissing a tear that clung to the corner of her eye. As though he'd read her mind, he assured her, "If you think I've got cold feet, the answer is no—and yes." She felt his hands curl around her wrist, lifting her fingers from beneath the rim of his pants. "Ice climber or not, my feet are damned cold." With a well-placed tongue taunting the bud of one upturned breast, he added huskily, "But I'm plenty warm everywhere else. Just thought we might be more comfortable in bed—or maybe even in your balmy refrigerator."

His low chuckle tickled her throat as he raised his head to place one lingering kiss on the rapid pulse of her throat. "What do you think?" he murmured, thrilling her as he nipped playfully at the tender skin.

She sighed, laying her cheek against his temple and closing her eyes. "If you can walk back to the cabin, now, then you've got more control than I do. But I suppose you're right."

With a hearty reluctance, she retied his sweatpants but couldn't resist a final, kittenish caress as she whispered, "You're not just a great big tease are you, Quaid?"

His chuckle was rich and tender as he reached up and began to dislodge the door above them. "You'll have to wait and see."

Her whole body glowed with his unspoken erotic vow that the best was yet to come. Because her mind was floating elsewhere, she barely registered the wild flurry of snow that invaded their haven as he pushed open the door.

After only a few seconds, he'd hoisted himself through the opening and was assisting her out of the four-wheeler. When he'd jumped to the ground and yelled that he'd catch her, a gust of wind dashed icy pellets into his good eye, blinding him as she jumped toward his arms.

When she collided with him, he fell back, landing them both in the snow, prone and laughing. "My hero," Val taunted as she settled atop his bare chest. "I don't think this is how damsels in distress are rescued in storybooks."

Encircling her with an arm, he kissed the tip of her nose. "Is that any way to talk about a handicapped man," he shouted over the stinging roar of the wind.

"Oh—" She blanched, noticing for the first time that he was blinking to clear his eye. "I'm sorry...."

He chuckled, hugging her to him. "Don't be. It's just that I'm bent over with lust. Terribly debilitating. Ask any man whom you've just had in your clutches."

Squinting up at her, he grinned, looking boyish and sexy. His expression was so endearing she couldn't help kissing both uplifted corners of his smile. "Poor crippled Quaid," she teased, running an impish hand along his inner thigh. "Give me an hour and I'll show you crippled."

With a hearty swat on her rump, he urged, "Let's get inside, or the sheriff's department will find us tomorrow morning, lying naked in the snow, looking like a very lewd popsicle." Nipping at her earlobe, he added, "Though I can think of worse ways to go..."

With a throaty giggle, Val allowed him to help her up. Hand in hand they sprinted toward the cabin, neither allowing themselves to dwell on what complications this night of abandon would cause, once the harsh light of day fell across their love-tossed sheets.

10

VAL HUDDLED before the fire, her ardor dampened by the chilly dash to the cabin. She looked down at herself—not exactly any sane man's idea of a femme fatale. She'd shed her parka. The snow on her fuzzy slippers was melting, leaving the pink footwear looking like drenched acrylic puppies. Sadly her navy knee socks weren't strictly textbook seduction gear, either.

Quaid had fed the fire, and it was blazing now. She hugged her knees, swathed beneath an ample green nightshirt. She grimaced as she saw herself the way Quaid would be seeing her momentarily, and she had an urge to dash into her bedroom and lock the door. But that was where she'd lured Billy Bob with a handful of squaw candy moments ago. She didn't want her overprotective dog getting the wrong idea about—well, anything that might take place before the fire that night.

Hearing the bathroom door open, she turned, her heart leaping. She thought she'd been nervous and self-conscious before, but seeing Quaid appear, backlit by the bathroom light, she caught her breath in awe.

He'd taken a shower and was clad only in a towel wrapped low over his hips, and he was carrying his shaving kit. His hair hung loose to just past his shoulders, giving him the look of a Viking warrior—and with the added eye patch, he seemed more like a mythological apparition than a mortal man.

As he came toward her, her eyes were drawn by the motion of strong muscles in his thighs, making his simple act of moving across the floor a spiritual experience.

His right calf caught her attention. On the inner side of his leg she could see several puckered scars and she frowned, recalling now that she'd seen a good deal of blood not only around his head, but around his legs as he lay in the snow that day long ago. It occurred to her that he must have been gored by the pointed crampons that had been fastened to his left boot.

"Not a pretty sight," he offered quietly as he took a seat beside her on the afghan she'd spread over the rug, laying the kit on the hearthstone. "And you thought you'd seen all my scars."

She turned to meet his ebony gaze. The twinkle was gone and his glance was tender yet intent, as though he were looking for any sign of retreat in her manner.

She leaned into his solidness, wiping away his apprehension, and he pulled her even closer within a harboring embrace. "That must have smarted," she responded, leaning her head on his chest.

His chuckle was low and without much humor. "A little."

"How are your feet? Warmer?" she asked, raising her eyes to his face.

"Much improved." He paused, lifting a querying brow. "And yours?"

"My poor fuzzies will never be the same."

"I meant—have your feet-gone cold?"

She shook her head, nuzzling the curling spring of hair on his chest. "If you mean, have I changed my mind—the answer's no." Slipping an arm about his taut waist, she asked, "You don't see Billy Bob anywhere, do you?"

His gaze narrowed with lazy amusement. "Where is she?"

"Happily tucked away on my bed."

His hand came out to stroke his knuckles along her jaw. "I'm gratified for your concern."

She smiled up at him, whispering, "I wouldn't want you to lose any important body parts."

"Any more, you mean...."

She kissed his knuckles as they came up to rub gently across her lips. "Right...."

After a quiet moment of gazing into the flames, Val shifted around to face him. With her back to the warmth of the fire and her hips grazing his, she lifted her hands to the wide expanse of his shoulders, admitting through a sigh, "You're a beautiful man, Quaid." She ran a strand of his towel-dried hair through her fingers, inhaling the fresh-washed fragrance. "I tried so hard to resist you." She smiled, and it held a measure of melancholy. "I'm glad I failed."

Her voice caught in her throat as his expression changed from soft amusement to a disturbing vulnerability.

"Oh—I didn't mean..." She rose up on her knees and brushed a brief kiss on his lips. "Don't worry that I'll cry foul tomorrow when it's over." She dusted another kiss across his mouth. "I want this Valentine's night with you. Let's not analyze it or find fault. Okay?"

"Happy Valentine's night—Valentine," he murmured as his arms came around her and he lowered her to his lap. "But just what makes you think—" he began as he ranged sultry kisses along her lips and throat "—this will be over tomorrow?"

She moaned, opening her lips to accept the intimacy

he was offering her, any spoken reply lost to a more urgent, age-old language.

Feeling a surge of new desire, Val encircled his chest with her arms, her hands spread and searching, exploring, memorizing every hard curve of him. So broad, so solid, his very maleness set her spiraling upward with a need to know him completely, and with an eagerness she'd never imagined possible.

She ran her hand through his hair, smoothing it back so that she could taste the lobe of his ear. She continued to stroke his hair, his temple. Then her hand found the patch that protected his eye and her fingers hovered there.

"Quaid," she whispered, "do you ever take this off?"

"Not in public," he said, his voice deep and rough. "It's not romantic, Val."

She could tell from the slight edge to his voice and the faint tensing of his body that he would be in no mood to make love to her if she insisted that he remove it—though she knew there would be nothing disgusting about his injury—not to her. But to protect his feelings, she left the subject alone. With one last tender kiss along the edge of the patch, she trailed her mouth down to meet his again, offering kisses that were deep and wet, pledging lush delights to come.

The fire crackled and hissed as wood smoke mingled with the tang of his shampoo and a fading reminder of the floral perfume she'd applied hours ago—before their fateful dinner confrontation. How implausible that now she was entwined within his embrace, her head supported in the crook of his arm as he gentled an exploring hand along her thigh.

His fingers were as light as angel's kisses as they quested upward, and Val gloried in his unhurried caress. His lips skimmed along her shoulder and moved lower to graze the rise of her breasts. She sighed and enfolded his head with her arms, pressing him even more deeply into her softness.

Without being aware of how it came to pass, Val found herself lying on her back with Quaid lounging across her, his towel-clad lap pressed to her thighs. When he lifted his head to gaze down at her, his long, straight hair grazed her cheeks. She nipped at the strands, loving the savage image he portrayed—a Viking—no doubt bent on stealing village virgins. The idea elicited a soft giggle that bubbled in her throat.

His loving expression grew quaintly confused as he lifted a quizzical brow. "What's so funny?" he murmured. "Am I so rusty at this that I'm laughable?"

"Not at all." She shook her head. "I was just thinking of myself as a virgin and you as a Viking who'd just stolen me from my plundered village."

He smiled softly. "Sounds like a fairly respectable fantasy to me. Want to play it out?"

She slid her hand around his shoulders. "You'd have to have a pretty good imagination to accept me—fuzzies, knee socks and thirty-something years old, as a comely village virgin." Her smile lost much of its fun. "Sorry I don't have any frilly clothes to help you fantasize—like Ginger's peekaboo bra...."

He tilted his head, eyeing her strangely. "Val," he murmured at last, dropping a kiss to her forehead and then on each flushed cheek. "Any man who would care to pretend that you're anything but the exciting, sexy woman that you are, wouldn't be worth your time." With that, he sat back on his haunches and tugged off first one of her slippers and then the next, laying them aside.

"I promise you," he continued as he began to slide

one of her knee socks down her leg, "that any man in town, given the choice of making love to you—socks and all—or Ginger in her naughty lace, would chose you and your socks."

The other scrap of navy wool disappeared. His hands had grazed her flesh only slightly, but the havoc his touch had created inside her was unbelievably intense. How magnificent he was—both physically and sexually. By his simple act of removing her socks, he was feeding a crazy, sweet urgency deep within her.

And as he began to remove her nightshirt, the lovely feeling seeped outward, engulfing her entirely in a heat that made her throb with the thrill of being desired.

By the time she lay beneath him, clad only in her panties, she felt beautiful and seductive. For she saw that erotic message in his hungry gaze.

Lowering his head, he grazed her belly with a kiss that was neither tentative nor halfhearted. And as his lips lovingly devoured her flesh, his fingers inched the last bit of cover down over her hips. With every touch, every murmured endearment, Val felt treasured, cherished. She closed her eyes, allowing tears of joy and disbelief to trail along her face unheeded. She would worry about the right or wrong of this tomorrow, but right now she could do nothing but revel in the wonder of it.

A wave of raw hunger and longing washed through her, sweeping away all pretense. With her tremulous sigh of anticipation, he tasted the sweet, damp nectar of her heightened passion.

She ceased to breathe, her body caught in a vortex of delight as Quaid feasted. She found herself growing light-headed and feared for a moment that she would faint. The feelings that he was eliciting within her were so wondrous as to be akin to pain, and she cried out, curling her fingers into his powerful shoulders. But at last, when she thought she could endure the bright, vast sensations no longer, instead of rending agony, she felt the beauty of release, and her body shuddered with rapture until, a timeless eternity later, she lay exhausted—consumed—glistening with spent ardor.

Quaid slid his head up to nestle himself on her belly to await the time when she would be ready for him again. He could wait. He knew that Val had been through a lot to reach the place where she was now, and to rush this thing between them might ruin the healing that she had begun this Valentine's night. She was finally reaching out, finally unmasked. And what he could see behind that mask was too fine to be allowed out of sight again.

He felt her fingers, trembly at first, begin to stroke his hair. "Quaid?" she whispered, her voice tinged with reverence.

He lifted his gaze to meet hers, but said nothing, not trusting his voice.

"Are you falling asleep?"

His smile was so soft, so loving, it was like a blow to her heart. "Is that what you want me to do?"

She smiled, unsure why she felt like some sheltered virgin at this moment—what a ridiculous thing to feel. But watching him through the shield of her lashes, her body still glowing, she felt as though she'd never been touched by a man before. Quaid's lovemaking was that extraordinary, that glorious. Almost timidly she touched his cheek. "I wonder if all Vikings make love as well as you?"

"Vikings?" His white teeth flashed in a quick grin. "I hate to disappoint you, but I come from Dutch-Irish immigrant stock."

"Take my word for it, Quaid," she assured him in a hushed tone, "there's Viking warrior in you."

Pushing himself up onto his hands and knees, he offered wryly, "I hope your insistence on playing out this Viking warrior fantasy doesn't put a strain on my—credibility."

Languidly she tugged away his towel, only to marvel at the embodiment of his passion. Relishing the lack of evident impairment, she whispered, "I wouldn't fret if I were you...." With a sigh of delighted anticipation, she drew his face to hers and opened her lips in a torrid invitation.

Quaid murmured against her lips. He kissed her deeply, then he drew slightly away. "Give this Viking a minute."

With her perplexed look, he lifted a brow. "Or do you want a Viking baby?"

She frowned. That problem hadn't occurred to her. She and John hadn't had much luck.... "You mean now? Well—no."

He lowered his lips to hers once again, murmuring, "Neither do I—now. That's why I need a minute."

Turning slightly away to his shaving kit, he discreetly slipped on protection before moving to blanket her with his body, again.

"I see you're a Boy Scout," she murmured. "Always prepared."

He chuckled at her unexpected joke. "Actually, I came to Valdez expecting to conquer ice, not village virgins. I found this kit under your bathroom sink."

She felt her face flame. "Oh—that must be Kal Martin's."

He raised a speculative brow. "I don't believe I've heard you mention Kal. I gather he's a good friend."

His face was close, and his half smile cautious. She

felt suddenly awkward lying there naked beneath Quaid, discussing another man's condoms. She wanted to explain. "He and his wife roomed with me last year during the festival. When Kal broke his foot climbing, they left rather hurriedly."

"What a shame," he murmured. Placing his hands on either side of her head, he smoothed her tangled curls. "I owe Kal a favor. I trust he can wait for his thank-you note, because I have a very pressing engagement at the moment."

Some basic female instinct prompted her to query sweetly, "Just what is that?"

His teeth flashed in devilish delight. "Oh, little virgin—what you're going to learn about Vikings..."

His kiss was heated yet gentle, taking away her breath as he settled over her. Smiling inwardly, she accepted him within her womanly core, wrapping her legs about her masterful plunderer as they slowly, delightfully became one being. Their moans mingled becoming the inflamed exultation of an otherworldly creature, a beautiful, unearthly beast, glistening and spiraling in a carnal dance of rebirth.

His loving left her throbbing from her parched, swollen lips to her flushed toes. She found herself clawing at his back, slickened by his heated arousal. His tongue teased and tormented her from the sensitive flesh of her ears to delicate, secret places that only lovers share. Her body quivered with wild elation at the discovery that this man could twist her, contort her at his whim—use her so brazenly, yet so exquisitely.

His hard, male lips moved against her fingers as he whispered her name, "Valentine..." Or had he said, "Be mine, Valentine...?" The murmured endearment dragged her to somewhere within the stark fringes of reality. Her throat so dry she could not speak, she lifted shaky fingers to his cheek, stroking the freshly shaven flesh, wishing she could be his but knowing she could not.

Pulling himself up beside her, he drew her into the crook of his arm and simply stared at her wordlessly for a long moment. Val, content in this wordless Valentine's fantasy, wanted time to cease, wanted to remain in Quaid's arms there beside the dying fire for the rest of eternity. She could see nothing before her in her life that could hope to surpass the reverence of this moment. But she couldn't bring herself to tell him how she felt. She knew, deep down, that this lapse of hers had been a terrible mistake, and unfair to Quaid. No matter what he thought about her expressing her guilt, she still couldn't allow herself to become emotionally dependent on anyone—to be anybody's Valentine.

"Did you hear me, Val?" he asked softly.

The mood suddenly broken, Val sighed sadly.

Quaid, hearing the unexpected sorrow, drew her gaze to his with a coaxing finger beneath her chin. "What was that for?"

She leaned against his shoulder, allowing her eyes to roam hungrily over his harshly beautiful face. "Oh—just reality setting in, I guess."

"Is it that bad?"

She shook her head. "Let's not talk about it now. I'm too tired to argue."

"Argue?" It was a surprised, whispered groan.

She swallowed, averting her gaze.

"I have no intention of arguing with you, Val." Undaunted, he slid on fresh protection. His hand traveled down to caress the inside of her thighs.

"Oh—but, Quaid…" she lamented, her body responding instantly. She was lost again—and so quickly. This man was shamelessly resourceful in his sexual prowess. Without the slightest intention, her lips sought his, and his mouth moved against hers, persuading, tempting, as his hands worked their magic.

She was a puppet in his clever hands, a slave to his every wish, and she delighted under his direction— losing sight of her fears and doubts. With her heart thumping wildly in her throat and chest, he gripped her hips, guiding himself home again. "What did you want to argue with me about?" he asked, his voice a labored whisper.

"Oh—Quaid…" she cried, her body soaring above the mundane, trivial problems of merely living her life. It didn't even bother her to realize she had no control over her own body when this man was lying naked above her. She was crazy, but it was just fine—just, absolutely wonderful. The thrill of his sexual abandon banished any other thought.

A fleeting, ironic smile crossed Quaid's mouth. Maybe he should have let her argue with him. Was repeatedly making love to her a sound idea? Was it anything short of addle-brained? He needed to fall in love with Valentine Larrabee like he needed to dive headfirst off Death Scream. And if history was any teacher, he very well could be signing his life away with tonight's foolish lack of restraint. But, even as his conscience battled with him, the sly devil on his shoulder whispered, "What man wouldn't trade his soul for one unmatched night of passion with you, Val?" Quaid had to give old Lucifer credit. He doubted that there would be many men who could resist such an angelic temptation as the woman who lay writhing and moaning with pleasure beneath him.

VAL HESITATED leaving the warmth of Quaid's sheltering body, but the fire was now nothing more than a few glowing embers and she was restless, needing to get away to think clearly. Her back was nestled against his chest, and his knees were drawn up behind hers. His arms held her securely to him. Even with him asleep, she knew that there would be no clear thinking where she was.

Doing her best not to awaken him, she gently lifted his arm and slid out of his all-encompassing embrace to scurry to her room and retrieve her terry robe. Much to her surprise, Billy Bob was hunkered down by the door instead of splayed across her bed as she'd expected.

As soon as she opened the door, her dog bounded out to make a quick inspection of the living room. Though Val tried to dissuade the dog, she had the effect of trying to dissuade a tidal wave. Billy Bob was immediately upon Quaid, sniffing and nudging at his prone body.

Swiftly she grabbed her robe and, shivering, slipped her arms into its immense sleeves. She was hurriedly tying the sash when she reentered the living room.

"Hello," Quaid offered, sounding drowsy.

Darting him a frightened look, she saw that he'd come up on his elbows. Billy Bob was sprawled out beside him, her head on his belly. "This isn't how I'd fantasized waking up."

Even in her disquiet, she had to smile—though weakly. "I'm sorry she woke you, Quaid. I was—" she faltered. What did she think she was going to tell him? That she was planning to work out some war plan to keep this from happening again? How could she say that to him just now? He looked so absolutely dear, his expression a sleepy mixture of confusion and amusement, his torso taut, broad and bronze in the glow of the doomed fire. Half of her wanted to crawl back under that afghan and know again the glory of his loving. But the other half of her knew better and was bound on keeping in control. Hoping her pause hadn't been overly long, she improvised, "I felt like a cup of hot chocolate. Want some?"

He frowned slightly and glanced at the wall clock, its luminous dial revealing the hard fact that it was nearly four in the morning. "Is anything wrong?" he queried, his insight far too well honed for a man who'd just been awakened by the big wet nose of a hairy beast.

She shrugged and painted on a smile. "What could be wrong?" With that, she grabbed up her fuzzies, now dry, and slipped them on. Not waiting for an answer, she hurried into the dark kitchen.

A few minutes later, as the milk heated on the stove, Quaid joined her. He'd also donned a robe. Close on his heels tramped Billy Bob.

"You want marshmallows in yours?" she asked lightly, avoiding direct eye contact. Just looking at him made her go mushy in the knees! She wondered how long this love-drugged feeling that he inspired would stay with her.

"No, thanks," he responded quietly. She heard him drag out a kitchen chair and sit down. "Do you want to talk about it?"

Dribbling chocolate syrup into the heated milk, she bit the inside of her cheek. Why was he going to insist on being direct? *Well*, she decided unhappily, *if he wants directness, I suppose that's what I'll have to give him.*

Without turning around, she began, "I don't want to talk about the lovemaking we shared, Quaid. I want to forget about it. Is that direct enough for you?"

She heard the chair scrape across the wood floor, and she knew he was rising to his feet. Seconds later, his hands were on her arms, turning her to face him. "I thought you said there would be no faultfinding, no crying foul."

She shook her head, dropping her gaze. "I'm not—I don't blame you—or me. I needed closeness, affection. I'm only human. It's just too bad I had to go about getting it in quite this way." She smiled sadly and shook her head again.

Quaid's hands slid gently up her arms to engulf her face, forcing her gaze back to meet his. "Don't close up on me, Val."

She faced him reluctantly, deciding to tell him the whole truth. With a fortifying intake of breath, she admitted, "You make love so beautifully, Quaid—more like a knight than a Viking. I could fall in love with you if I'm not careful. I'm vulnerable that way right now— any caring speech, any soft glance and I'm putty."

"That's not true," he countered, his expression growing dark. "What about Ross and the others. Don't tell me you haven't had your share of caring speeches and soft glances tossed your way."

"Well—I didn't mean I was *loose!*" she contradicted tightly. "You—you're so—so strong and in control. I guess I'm drawn to you because I'm such a mess...."

His jaw tightened as she continued. "Maybe I thought that making love with you would somehow inject me with some of your steel. Oh, I don't know...."

His lips lifted sardonically. "Inject? Very appropriate word choice, I'd say, considering everything." He dropped his arms to his side, releasing her. "I don't know what to say."

She saw the hurt in his gaze and felt bereft when his touch was suddenly gone. A wayward part of her longed to feel his hands on her face again, to know the rough yet silky feel of his chest, the potency of his loins between her yielding thighs.

Deep in her belly she felt desire grow again and cursed herself. Here he was, not touching her, just looking at her, his expression somber yet piercingly sweet, and she was floundering, lost to any intelligent arguments on the subject of Quaid Perrault.

Turning away, she shut off the stove and lay the syrup bottle aside before facing him again. When she did, she took his hand and walked with him from the kitchen. Silently she led him past Billy Bob, who'd taken up her post on the couch.

When they'd crossed the threshold into her bedroom, Quaid asked her in a voice that was very doubtful, "Where are you taking me?"

She closed the door behind them before she whispered, "Quaid, let me have this night with you, then let me handle my life—my way. Will you promise me that?"

Her entreaty was painful to hear, but her voice had told him that it had also been painful to say. Knowing that he too had no business drawing out this love affair, considering his situation, he had to admit that she was probably right. Lifting her into his arms, he asked, "Will you promise me that you won't retreat into your guilt? You must realize that your reaction to your husband's defeatist attitude was completely human."

For a moment there was silence. And because his eyes were slow to adjust to the pitch-darkness of her bedroom, he couldn't detect her expression. Finally she curled her arms about his neck and pressed a kiss on his jaw, whispering, "Thank you, Quaid."

Her lips trailed along to find his mouth, and she kissed him lightly again. "You're a very special man."

Carrying her to her bed, he lowered her to the spread and joined her there, murmuring, "I'm a very lucky man...at least, for tonight."

11

BY MORNING both Val and Quaid realized that they had embarked on an affair that couldn't be turned off merely because it wasn't a sound idea. They craved each other too much to be wise, and they exulted in the erotic release they had found together.

Though they knew this truth in their heads, they were reluctant to admit it in their hearts. Neither one of them had wanted this to happen. Val had learned that to love someone meant gambling that you might not be loved in return—someday—for some failing, either physical or mental. She didn't want to become vulnerable to Quaid by falling in love with him and then, one day, discover that she had become a burden.

He was also feeling vulnerable emotionally. The last thing on earth he'd wanted to do on this trip to Valdez was become preoccupied with someone. Unfortunately, it was too late now. He was involved with Val. He'd reached out to her as a friend, knowing the risks; one can't really be a friend without becoming involved. But he'd had no idea where that commitment would ultimately lead. Had he realized they'd end up in bed and that he'd fall in love with her, he didn't know what he would have done. Probably the exact same thing. *Damn his stupid timing.*

Looking at her now, so flushed and silent, sitting across from him at the breakfast table, he couldn't suppress a gentle smile. They'd loved each other well and thoroughly last night—or more correctly, all night. He didn't know how they would fare today on the ice.

As she took a sip of her coffee, he asked, "Sleepy?"

She avoided his gaze, but her cheeks pinkened. "I was just wondering the same thing about you." Finally her eyes met his. "I'm not sure I'll be able to stay awake today."

He laughed, and the rich sound of it warmed her through and through. "If I recall correctly, there's a rock ledge on the second pitch. We could—"

"I know what we could do," she interrupted, her eyes glistening with a mixture of remembered passion and embarrassment. "And how would we explain it to Ross?"

Lifting a sardonic brow, he offered, "I'd forgotten Ross was going to go with us today."

She stood to remove her plate to the sink. "I hate to have to remind you of this, but we have no transportation. Ross is our ride to the canyon."

Quaid joined her at the sink. After putting his dishes in to soak, he moved up behind her, enfolding her fully against him. Nuzzling her ear, he suggested softly, "Maybe we ought to call him back and tell him we have the flu."

She could feel exciting evidence of his arousal against her hips, and her reaction was intense. Leaning into his potent warmth, she sighed, savoring the moment. Her body grew damp, pulsing with heated desire for him.

Lifting her head, she grazed his jaw with a kiss, murmuring, "If this is the flu, then I don't look forward to getting well."

Turning her in his arms, he lowered his lips to hers, and very quickly they were swept away by their fiery passions for each other. Her arms curled about his neck and wrapped him tightly as his hands caressed, searched and roamed, his trek over her yielding body delighting them both.

Without warning, there was a loud rapping on the cabin's front door, and Billy Bob went into a mindless fit of barking as she scampered to the door, scratching and snarling.

Ross had arrived.

"Shut up, dawg!" their friend called from the front porch. "I've brought some squaw candy to soothe your savage breast!"

Val slowly released Quaid, and they gazed at each other for a pained minute before she said, "I think I'd better get that before Billy Bob eats the door."

Quaid patted her hip, murmuring hoarsely, "I think I'd better retreat to the bathroom to—er—recover."

She smiled shyly, still in awe of his sexual power over her, and apparently, hers over him. Without another word she headed toward the front door. She gave Quaid time to retire to the bathroom before she let Ross in.

"Hi, Val," he nearly shouted, appearing in robust spirits. "Here's a peace offering for…" In the midst of handing her a bag of dried salmon for Billy Bob, he stopped speaking and just stared at her.

"What's the matter?" she asked after an awkward pause, nervously smoothing back her mussed hair.

He shook his head, handing her the bag. "Nothing— it's just that you look so—so radiant this morning." Pulling off a glove, he touched her cheek. "Your face is hot. Are you feeling okay?"

She laughed tautly. "Do I have to be sick to look radiant?"

He smiled, but the pleasant expression didn't quite

stifle the befuddled look in his eyes. "I guess I should have said 'flushed'—but no less radiant."

Taking the bag, she swung around toward the kitchen. "Nice recovery, Ross. But, to answer your question, I'm fine—just a little tired. I—I didn't sleep well."

"Where's old Quaid? Still in bed?"

"I'm right here," Quaid provided, coming out of the bathroom, appearing cool and collected. "You're certainly prompt this morning."

"Any reason I shouldn't be?" Ross looked down at his watch. "It's nine o'clock. We need to get on the ice if we're going to finish before dark." Motioning over his shoulder toward the front of the cabin, he commented, "Sorry to hear about the mishap last night, Quaid. Thought you could handle a four-wheel drive better than that. Lucky you were so near home."

Quaid shrugged, and Val was relieved to note that he didn't glance her way as he responded, "Icy roads can be unpredictable."

"Yeah, I guess." He turned to Val, who'd busied herself feeding Billy Bob some of Ross's gift. "You two about ready to go?"

"Absolutely," Quaid said, heading up the stairs two at a time. "Just let me get my backpack."

When he'd disappeared, Ross turned a jaundiced eye toward Val and asked under his breath, "Everything okay with you two?"

She met his gaze with misgivings. "Sure—we're getting along fine." Well, she mused, that wasn't a lie, anyway. She just hoped that Ross didn't ask anything more direct. She had the feeling the dreaded question was right on the tip of his tongue.

"Val, why do I feel like I've walked in on—"

"Ross," she interjected, her voice a bit stiff. "Thanks for the dried salmon."

It had come out sounding like "mind your own business," so Ross merely nodded and mumbled, "Okay, okay."

Quaid came loping down the stairs carrying his backpack and a harness filled with ice tools and hammers. With a quick grin that gave away nothing of his frustration, he said, "Looks like it's going to be a beautiful day for climbing."

"Yeah," Ross agreed, though his expression was closed in speculation.

"Well," Val added with a barely detectable sigh, "since we agree it's a beautiful day for climbing, let's get going."

"I can't wait," Quaid said. It sounded a little tight.

"Neither can I," Val added, casting him a regretful glance. His expression mirrored hers. The last thing either of them wanted to do was head out that cabin door to spend hours draining their already depleted energies on anything less fulfilling than climbing between tousled sheets and making each other delirious.

"Me, too," Ross chimed in, resuming his original cheerful air.

Val had just locked her door. She darted her friend a puzzled look. "You too, *what*, Ross?"

He looked from her to Quaid, and then back to her, wondering where her mind had gone. "Me too, *what*?" he asked incredulously. "Why, I'm looking forward to climbing. That *is* what we were talking about, isn't it?"

"Oh?" Val felt her face flush again, amazed at her lack of concentration lately—at least when Quaid was within touching distance. "I guess—me, too. How about you, Quaid?"

"Can't wait," he repeated halfheartedly as he trudged off toward Ross's pickup.

Ross frowned, muttering under his breath, "This is where I came in." Shaking his head, he muttered sarcastically, "Hell! This is going to be a *stimulating* day— as long as I talk to myself."

Quaid and Val said nothing; they merely exchanged pained glances at Ross's choice of words. They were agonizingly aware of a more stimulating way they might have spent the day.

THE WEEK OF THE FESTIVAL progressed well. All their climbs were intoxicating—almost as much as Quaid's expertise in their shared bed. Neither Quaid nor Val found it necessary to discuss climbing Death Scream during the next four days, both of them thinking the subject was settled.

On the evening before the final day, Quaid casually remarked, "I talked to Doug Randall today. He said he'd be happy to have you go with him tomorrow."

Val replaced her hairbrush on her dresser and turned to smile at the man who was lounging naked on her bed, the sheet drawn up to preserve only scant decency along the lower curve of his hip. "Doug Randall?" she asked. "Where would I want to go with him?"

He patted the bed. "Come here."

Gladly accepting his invitation, she shrugged off her robe and climbed, nude, beneath the covers, laying her head on his chest. "Mmm," she sighed, inhaling his familiar scent. "I thought this day would never end. But it was fun, wasn't it? We're really working as a team now."

"Yes. And we're not too bad on the ice, either," he

whispered, his hand stroking seductively along her ear.

"Oh, you…" She laughed, running her fingernails languidly through the silky hair on his chest. "Did anyone ever tell you you're a sex maniac?"

"Not so far today. You?"

She shook her head, luxuriating in the erotic messages of his hands. "Never. I'm the ice queen of Valdez, or haven't you heard?"

His deep chuckle sent a thrill through her as he drew up a leg to lay across both of hers. "If you're Valdez's ice queen, I'd like to meet the local hot mamma."

The hand that was caressing his chest dipped down, and she ran a finger playfully through the narrowing band of hair that graced his belly. "You would, would you," she queried, her lips tasting his flesh. "You're tired of ice queens?"

He cupped a hip, pressing her more firmly against his groin. "There are times when I'm damn exhausted."

She felt his readiness and sighed contentedly. "But not right now, I notice."

"Oh—sweetheart, you have no idea."

"You will let me know when you tire of me," she teased, but something in the back of her mind clicked with memory and she stiffened, her whole being listening intently for his response.

"I may tire because of you, but not *of* you—never *of* you.…" He kissed the top of her head and slid over to blanket her body.

"You can't know that for certain, Quaid. No one can."

He paused in the act of kissing each quivering eyelid. "I can, Val." He smoothed back a stray lock of her hair and then kissed the place where it had been. "I can—because I love you. That's all I need to know." He didn't add that this wasn't a good thing to admit the very night before he was to climb Death Scream. But, he couldn't keep from saying it to her any longer.

His love for her was a very real entity in his life now, and something he would have to deal with as he had everything else in his life—head-on. His falling in love with her had come at a difficult time and might be a problem tomorrow. But as long as he didn't have to worry about her being along, he felt he would be strong enough to finish the climb.

Her eyes shot open. Her deepest fears had just come true! *Oh, God, please!* she cried inwardly. *He can't mean this!* Unable to find words to express her absolute rejection of the idea, she stared at him.

He smiled down at her. "Does it really surprise you that I've fallen in love with you?"

Her expression anxious, she stammered, "I—I suppose it occurred to me. I told you that first morning I thought you were ready for a relationship."

"I remember."

"And I told you I wasn't."

There was a pause and she glimpsed confusion in his gaze. "I remember that, too." His handsome, damaged face clouded. "Are you telling me you don't love me?"

The fringe of her lashes fluttered and dropped, shadowing her eyes. What could she say to him? What, but the awful truth. "You have a right to something better than I can offer," she whispered miserably. "For years I've managed to live tolerably well without real emotion—"

"Val, that wasn't living," he admonished. "The greatest tragedy in life is to give up on yourself. I won't let you do that."

"What do you know about giving up?" she asked

glumly, her desire gone, crushed beneath the weight of her guilt and fear. "I hate it when you think you know how I feel." Pressing against his chest, she slid far enough away to be free of his scent and his touch. *Oh, why couldn't we have just made love instead of having to ruin everything with useless talk!*

Covering herself as best she could with a corner of the sheet, she added with the brusqueness of a person close to tears, "You didn't know how I felt when I told you I was going to climb Death Scream, and you don't know what I'm feeling now."

She favored him with a hurt glance that was almost a dare for him to argue with her. He didn't. Instead, he propped himself up on an elbow and smiled, refusing to be daunted. "A lot has happened since then," he reminded her softly. "And you made the right decision not to climb Death Scream."

She stared at him, her eyes growing round. "What?" she demanded in a rough whisper. "What makes you think I've changed my mind? I thought you understood I'd be going along."

Quaid's smile faded and he sat up. Now it was his turn to stare at her. Impatience laced his tone as he prodded, "Tell me you're kidding. This is a damned joke, right?"

"Not at all!" Her cheeks flaming, she lowered her eyes, only to lift them again as she heaved a sigh of exasperation. "Don't fight me on this, Quaid. I'm good. All week you've been telling me I'm good!"

His gaze grew cold as he searched her animated face. "Hell—you're actually serious...."

At the realization, he dashed the sheet away from him, yanking it from Val's fingers as he did so. Jumping from the bed, he towered over her quailing body, the image of an angry Norse god. His mane, long, wild and dark, swirled in manly disarray about his broad shoulders. His swarthy gaze hardened to obsidian in the semidarkness. Even within the profanity of his marred features, his face was stirring.

She almost believed he could reach up and snatch lightning from the sky. He was angry enough to run her through with such a weapon had there been any lightning at his disposal. Fortunately, the sky was clear, leaving her illusory god without a lethal weapon—unless one considered his lovemaking to be lethal, she thought wretchedly.

His voice, lowered to a subdued growl, drew her from her dark fancy. "Dammit to hell, Val. I'd hoped our relationship had grown beyond this competitive bull."

His cutting words injected steel into her spine and she countered, "It isn't competitive bull. I have to do this. I told you why!"

Raking his fingers through his hair, he fought for reason. "Val, your reaction to your husband's death was perfectly normal. Ninety-nine percent of the people in the world would react as you did." Frustration sparkled in the brightness of his ebony gaze as he strove for calm. "Nobody blames you for what happened to John—least of all, John. Forget this crazy scheme—forget it, now!"

A cowardly urge to turn and run crawled up her spine, but with great effort, her voice was cool and composed. "I won't forget it. I'm going with you."

"No, you're not." There was a deadly finality in his tone. "It's foolish. You have nothing to prove."

"If I don't have anything to prove, then just what do you think you have to prove?"

He blanched. "That I can finish it."

"Well, that's certainly all I need to hear!" She

laughed sarcastically. "No, I'll tell you what you have to prove—some sort of macho bull—to pull off your 'hardest of the hard men' coup." Anger lent ice to her tone, covering her anxiety. "If you insist on following through for *that* trivial reason, then I plan to climb with you."

"You don't know what you're talking about."

"*I* don't?" she cried, her voice a disbelieving echo. "I'm not the one who broke every bone in my body and was almost blinded!"

She watched his face go white, and she felt a painful catch in her heart at his stark reaction to her remark. Though she'd wanted to be hard and fiercely aggressive, his anguished expression dampened her resolve. Unable to help herself, she softened her tone and found herself pleading sadly, "Do you really know what *you're* talking about?"

There was a rigidness in the muscles of his body, and for a second she thought she saw some dreadful emotion in his dusky gaze—something that made her shudder. What had it been, and why did she have the utterly absurd feeling that she'd seen terror lurking there?

12

Quaid towered above her, gloriously naked yet utterly distant. His body, minutes ago so sheltering and stimulating, now seemed as inflexible as granite.

The odd, alarmed look she'd seen flash across his face was gone, or perhaps she'd imagined it. In its place there was nothing but cold rejection—something Val had never seen in him before. It frightened and confused her, doing more damage than a sharp slap across her face.

The pang of his emotional retreat as he turned his back and strode from her bedroom was hard to take. She sat fixedly on her knees, clutching sheets still warm from the brush of his skin, still redolent with his scent. Under her stiffened fingers, the fabric cooled, and she could only stare at the closed door, registering his unexpected abandonment as importantly as the moment she'd realized her parents were lost to her beneath the mangled earth.

She shivered, at last finding the ability to stir from her stupor. With ponderous movements, she shifted to the side of the bed to retrieve her robe from the vanity bench. She was not accustomed to sleeping in the nude—not until Quaid's entrance into her sexual life. She smiled ruefully at the mere suggestion that before Quaid had come along, she'd even *had* a sexual life. To be honest, she couldn't really call what she and John had shared particularly awe inspiring—even before his illness. Though, thanks to Quaid, she'd only found that out recently.

Listless, she rummaged in a drawer, searching for a nightshirt and some long socks. She certainly didn't need to look fetching tonight. Quaid had made it clear that he wanted nothing to do with her.

Pulling on a pair of red wool socks and shucking her robe to don a mauve nightshirt, she climbed unhappily between her sheets. Just as she'd settled within the blankets, she became aware that Billy Bob was scratching at her door. Heaving an exasperated sigh, she threw off the covers and padded across the room and let her dog in.

"What did he do, cast you off, too?" she mumbled as her pet scampered to her bed and bounded onto it, making the springs cry out in protest.

"No, you don't," Val groused, sliding back between the sheets and shoving her dog with her hip. "Move over. This is my bed, you know. Besides, I'm not in the mood to cuddle." That was a lie. All she wanted in the world was to snuggle against Quaid and sleep peacefully. All she wanted was for him to hold her in his arms, happy that she planned to join him on the historic climb tomorrow.

She squeezed her eyes shut, admonishing herself to fall asleep. She needed to rest. Tomorrow was the big day, and she was damn well not going to allow Quaid's silent intimidation to force her to back down. She had just as much riding on this climb as he did.

QUAID STOOD NAKED before the fire, staring at the dying flames. He could see very clearly the bleak calamity that tomorrow portended, and a shiver ran through him. In his mind he saw again the one-hundred-story-high latticework of delicate blue icicles, intermingled with nasty, insubstantial devil's club, a diabolical shrub that lurked among the thin shards of ice along Death Scream's route. It would tease the unwitting climber with a promise of a helping hand, but in truth, the brush harbored painful spurs.

To grab at devil's club in haste or panic could be tragic. The spines would pierce glove, palm and bone, and if the climber was not well protected, and in need of a handhold, the damned bush could easily be uprooted, and aid only in following the hapless victim earthward in a wailing, screaming somersault through uncompromising sky. Along the way, other shoots of devil's club lay in ambush, their claws outstretched to shred skin as the doomed climber sped downward. Suddenly in his imagination, Quaid saw Val in trouble, crying out in pain, falling, tumbling. Instinctively he reached for her, in his protective rashness bashing his fist against the mantel.

With a curse, he ran his scraped knuckles across his scarred chin, recalling his own plunge through flesh-rending devil's club. He discovered his fist was shaking and stared down at his hands. He blinked stupidly, uncomprehending. He had big hands. Strong hands with long, narrow fingers—and they were trembling as though he were ancient and palsied. Some slim thread that had been holding him together snapped inside him, and a low, thwarted moan tore from his throat. *Hell*, he was so terrified he no longer had control over his own hands.

"Damn you, you stupid coward..." he berated himself, his fingers curling into angry fists in his hair. He clenched until his scalp ached, trying to regain control with physical pain—something he understood and could handle. But it was no use.

His gnawing terror had finally drained him of all

pretense, of all his waning mental discipline. Now, naked and very alone, with rage and terror slicing through his body, he had nowhere to turn. He was lost, helpless in his fear for himself and for the damnable, wonderful, foolish woman he loved.

The powerful muscles in his legs gave way, and he found himself crumpling to his knees before the fire. With dread overcoming him, hard, burning sobs raked his soul and blistered his throat. The undulating flames grew dim, blurring before him, and, for the first time in his life, Quaid Perrault cried.

VAL DRAPED HER ARM across her eyes and sighed aloud. She wouldn't be able to sleep; she knew it. There was no use even trying. Swinging her legs over the edge of the bed, she slid her feet into her fuzzies and pulled her robe on. She might as well get in a little practice signing for the deaf. She'd let that project go for the past two weeks, and she was already getting rusty.

Irritably she wondered how to sign troglodyte, as she shuffled to her door. "Troglodyte, ogre, jerk…" she muttered, yanking open her door and striking out around the practice ladder toward the living area. "Or even better, son of a—" Her gaze dropped, hit Quaid's slumped form and gripped like a vise. "My God…" she whispered, unable to comprehend what she was seeing. A rosy heat began to scorch her cheeks like slap marks. She felt the sting of her own flesh as understanding slowly dawned. *Quaid was crying.*

She had become immobile, clinging to the last tattered strands of her rebellion. But the sight of his distress made her go clammy inside and coldly sick in her stomach. The fire backlit his hunched figure. His shoulders had been shaking, his hands hiding his face.

Having heard the door to her room slam shut, he

jerked around to see the shock gleaming in her wide eyes as she watched him crouching there—*caught*—unstrung to his soul.

His face—Quaid's proud, ravaged face—was too stricken to gaze upon, but Val couldn't pull her eyes away. Though she wanted to spare him the embarrassment of being found in such a terrible, vulnerable way, she couldn't withdraw her eyes from his face: blighted, wary, yet unutterably beautiful.

She felt as though she were choking on her own breath. She had never seen this man before. He was a stranger hunched there, a stranger in great pain. *Why?* She'd thought him so strong, so invincible. How could he be crying?

Her defiant posture crumpled, and she moved like a sleepwalker toward him. "Quaid? What is it?" She was surprised she could get the words through the paralyzing fear that blocked her throat.

Pushing himself up unsteadily, he stood to face her—naked, physically perfect even with his scars. His broad chest rose and fell in agitation, and his face was white, as leached as his precious, bedeviling Death Scream. Her heart battered at the walls of her chest in her concern. Reaching out to him, she placed her palm on his chest.

A grimace twisted his features at her touch. Ashamed that she had witnessed the gutless wonder that he was, Quaid cursed himself beneath his breath and lurched away.

Covering with a bitter laugh, he sneered, "Hell, Val, what makes you think there's anything wrong?"

Twisting away, he leaned his head back to stare up at the ceiling. Exhaling slowly, he propped his fists on his hips. His shoulders were straight, his long, sinewy legs braced wide. *Strength* was the message his body screamed, *strength and power*. Though his stance was both intimidating and calculating, there was nothing honest about it. The truth lay in one telltale sign that Quaid didn't even realize he was broadcasting—the anxious flexing and unflexing of one fist.

Quaid was magnificent even in his despair, beautifully unselfconscious of his nakedness. Yet he was determined to hide some awful truth from her with this empty farce, even now.

Val may have been slow to see that he had a problem—or possibly just slow to face the fact—but she was not foolish enough to let this thing go. He was the most guarded man she'd ever met—with high, protective walls about his heart. But damn her if she didn't try to scale them, try to reach him.

"You must think I'm an idiot, Quaid," she murmured toward his rigid back.

"I think you're a fool." His voice was hoarse, pained, giving away more than his intractable stance. "But then I'm a fine one to cast stones. I'm the one who had to fall in love with you."

She was dumbfounded. "I—I don't understand...."

"Understand this, then. I'm not climbing Death Scream tomorrow."

He'd uttered the vow so wretchedly, sounding so resigned—as though he felt he'd failed in some terrible way. She had to know what had caused such a radical change of heart. "But Quaid..." She held her hands wide, in a beseeching gesture, though he couldn't see her. *"Why?"*

He shook his head. "I've accepted the fact that I could die, but I can't accept the fact that you could—" his were the words of a stricken man "—that I could kill you if I screw up."

"But you won't," she insisted. Wanting to help, to

put him at ease, she edged closer. "You're an expert climber. You have nerves of steel. If you weren't so strong I might not feel that I could do it, but—"

"Nerves of *steel?*" He cast her words back at her as though they were sour on his tongue. Without warning, he grabbed the fireplace poker and, grinding out a vile curse, flung it across the room. It clattered loudly along the floor and came to a thudding stop against the front door. "What the hell do you know, Val?" he growled through clenched jaws. He spun to face her, his black hair whipping the air and settling wildly about his tensed face and shoulders. "I'm scared to death, sweetheart! Your big, brave hero is nothing but a fake, a quivering, slobbering—" His voice faltered, and his fists went up to his temples. An anguished, devastating howl issued up from his throat, the tortured sound of something wild and wounded.

Quaid spared himself nothing, left himself no pride behind which to hide. He sank to one knee, catching himself with a fist on the wooden planks, which had the look and sound of an angry punch. His shoulders slumped wearily. Propping his forearm across his knee, he opened and closed the abused hand in taut frustration.

Val was knocked senseless by the sudden storm of his anguish. She could do nothing but stare at him, at the long, sinewy muscles of his body, narrowed hips and broad shoulders, so potent yet brought low by something that was to Quaid, horrible and unspeakable. No longer Thor, the all-powerful god of thunder, the Quaid Perrault that knelt before her was a shattered mortal man.

She could see terrific tension thrumming along his muscles and wanted to find words to comfort him. Seeing him like this, tears welled unheeded in her eyes.

Quaid was older than his thirty-six years in many ways, yet in others he was younger. It was the youth she saw now, the youth who'd always been so lonely, so needy. The sight of his suffering wrung her heart.

She moved to him and dropped to her knees to place a protective arm about his wide shoulders. "Quaid, why didn't you tell me? I had no idea what this climb was costing you. I thought..." Her lips trembled and she had to pause to control her voice. "I guess, I don't exactly know what I thought." Biting her lip, she watched him, watched his harsh profile. After a long moment, she whispered, "I think I'm ready to take on your devil with you, Quaid. Please let me."

She watched the muscles in his jaw bunch and flex for a long time before he finally glanced over at her, his expression grim. He opened his mouth to speak, but no words came. He cleared his throat, fumbled for words and then, with a wince at his ineptness, shifted his gaze away.

With her encouraging tug on his arm, he stood, and they walked together to the couch. Handing him the afghan, she offered quietly, "Aren't you cold?"

His breathing was ragged as he faced her. "I don't feel much at all," he finally said, dragging a corner of it across his lap for modesty's sake.

Reaching up, she wiped a tear from his cheek.

Embarrassed, he took her hand away, but Val was having no more of his rejection. She took his hand, forming a warm sphere around it with both of hers. "Talk to me, Quaid," she urged him.

There was tragic unhappiness in his gaze as he met her eyes, and she knew that unguarded expression was destined to haunt her for the rest of her days.

"I'm a stupid ass, Val," he admitted thickly, feeling it in his soul. "You don't want to hear this."

He averted his gaze, but with her gentle squeeze of his fingers, he faced her once more.

She smiled weakly, hearteningly, because her throat was aching so with pain for him that she couldn't speak.

After the silence had run some unexplainable, necessary course, Quaid began, his mouth tight with purpose. "Lylith—my ex-wife—loved the power and money that surrounded what I did," he began, his voice rough and almost too quiet for her to hear.

When he paused, she nodded to encourage him. "Go on."

"Lylith hated the ice climbing. She grudgingly put up with it. Thought it was a phase, I suppose. But that February, we were invited to take a cruise on a friend's yacht. I told her to go without me, that I'd join her when they docked at Saint Thomas. It was a Valentine cruise, and it happened to conflict with the Ice Festival." He glanced down at Val's hands holding his. Her fingers were so small, so cool. He had the urge to kiss each finger in its turn. Fighting it, knowing he had to get this said, he went on. "Lylith blew up. She told me she hated my climbing, that I'd kill myself one day and she didn't intend to hang around and watch me do it."

Val gazed at his face in awe. His furrowed brow, his closed features were bewitching as he recounted the events. "She left me," he stated bluntly. "I don't know if she went on the cruise. I don't know if she ever came to see me in the hospital. If she did, it was during the weeks when I was in a coma."

"And she never visited you later?" Val asked, her tone disbelieving.

"Lylith never liked hospitals much," he muttered, making excuses for his wife that she didn't deserve. "Anyway, when I came to Valdez that year, I was miserable about her leaving. My mind wasn't on the climb and I made mistakes—stupid mistakes."

His lips twisted in an ironic smile. "Hell, I can't blame her for walking out. I didn't take much time off to be with her. And thinking back on it, I was a real jerk to expect her to go on a Valentine cruise alone. I was every bit the ass she told me I was—a cocky ice junkie, full of my own damned importance. Thought I could climb Death Scream alone no matter what my mental state might be—big, brave stud on the ice. Then when I was, quote—*the hardest of the hard men*—unquote, she'd forget everything and come running back to me." He snorted with self-revulsion. "I was a macho bastard."

Val felt everything inside her fuse into one warm, hard knot as she watched him, heard his unhappy confession. She was surprised to discover that she felt oddly at peace, wholly in his corner, even after having witnessed him in all his self-loathing.

She'd resented John for his weakness. What was it now that made her want to take Quaid in her arms and hold him, love him, tell him that everything would be all right? She hadn't thought she could ever actually *want* to comfort a frightened man again. Maybe it was because Quaid was battling his fear. Maybe that was the difference between John and Quaid. It was human to be afraid. It was only cowardice when one refused to confront the fear.

"I screwed up because I was distracted, worried about her," he acknowledged, breaking through her thoughts. He cast his gaze toward the ceiling and then shook his head wearily. "I covered with a lot of bragging, drinking and coming on to women, but I was dead inside. I'd failed at my marriage—couldn't hold on to *my* woman." His lip curled with disgust. "Me—stupid schmuck—Tarzan." Turning his hand over both of hers, he squeezed them. "I never thought I'd ever admit that to a living soul."

There were tears in her eyes, and his somber face blurred. "I'm glad you told me."

Taking both of her hands in his, he groaned plaintively, "I've got to climb Death Scream, Val. I've got to get back my self-respect. But I can't if I have to worry about you, too." His glistening gaze was eloquent in its plea. "I can't let anything happen to you. I wouldn't want to live if I thought I'd caused you to be hurt."

Quaid was by nature a strong, aggressive man who simply could not accept defeat, could not allow a damnable wall of ice to conquer him. He'd battled long and hard to get to this place. Until now, she'd had no idea how long and how difficult that battle had been.

She couldn't pretend to understand why he thought he would be less than wonderful if he didn't make this climb. But for Quaid, his need to defeat Death Scream was as undeniable as her love for him. The revelation that she was in love with Quaid didn't even surprise her. One day she would think back about Quaid— about meeting him. She'd probably find that she'd been in love with him when she'd rescued him after his fall, so brave, so valiant in his struggle to live. Yet, what difference did it make anymore *when* she'd actually fallen in love with him? Right now, it only mattered that she had.

She regretted the fact that she hadn't been there for him to lean on before tonight. He'd been carrying around this dreadful terror, hiding it from her because she'd been reticent to allow herself to become emotionally close. Because she'd chosen to wallow in her guilt, she'd cheated them both.

It was suddenly very clear to her that she didn't have to climb Death Scream to feel at peace with herself. Just knowing she had the power, even the desire, to comfort another human being again was enough...for now. Besides, to insist on climbing would be cruel and dangerous for Quaid—and for Ross.

Swallowing a tender lump that had formed in her throat, she gathered him close, loving him so, and was silent, content to merely hold him.

When she could speak steadily, she promised, "You and Ross climb Death Scream tomorrow, darling. I'll be waiting. You don't have to worry about me."

He stiffened for a moment, as though in disbelief. But in a matter of a few heartbeats, she felt his arms tighten about her. "*God*, Val," he muttered against her cheek. "Thank you."

He drew her face to his. His kiss was so filled with ardent emotion, it overwhelmed her. When he lifted his head to graze the tip of her nose with his lips, she whispered raggedly, "Don't you think you should get to bed?"

He lowered his head so that he could look directly into her shimmering eyes. With a concerned voice that was soft velvet, he asked, "Are you tired?"

"I was thinking of you."

"What a coincidence," he murmured against her throat. "I always seem to be thinking of you."

Relieved, tremulous laughter wavered against his temple. "This is for your own good, Quaid," she admonished as she wriggled reluctantly from his embrace. "Go on upstairs and get some rest."

His face clouded, and he appeared charmingly wounded. "Can't we even sleep together?"

She lifted a doubtful brow and stood. "Would we sleep?"

He shrugged, his expression a touching mixture of both boyish and very grown-up charms.

"That's what I thought." Pointing toward his loft, she ordered softly, "I want you well rested. I have plans for you *after* tomorrow."

With that, she disappeared into her bedroom, leaving her winsome, warm-natured image behind. Quaid found himself smiling after her and feeling almost light-headed. Valentine Larrabee loved him, loved him enough to let him make the climb without her. She'd made quite a sacrifice, he realized. What a woman she was.

Shaking his head at the irony of his good luck, he pushed himself up, still feeling a little shaky. Who would have guessed that breaking down in front of Val the way he had would free him of the torture festering in his soul?

She was the last person in the world he'd wanted to find out about his weakness. Yet she had lifted a great weight from his shoulders, this fragile-looking, brave woman of gentleness and passion. His glance caught on the poker that lay against the front door, and he pulled a hand through his hair. What a bastard he'd been tonight. But Val hadn't even flinched. She'd just reached out her small, merciful hand and taken his: big, callused and trembling. And she loved him—even after seeing him crumple into a destroyed heap on her rug—she loved him.

He shuddered to think how he must have looked, cowering there on his knees. Shaking his head in perplexed awe, he mumbled, "Perrault, you don't deserve her. You're a lucky one-eyed bastard." He moved slowly up the steps, repeating, "*Damned* lucky." Tomorrow—if his luck held—he would prove himself—to himself, and he'd be whole again.

A FEW MINUTES LATER, Val heard a light tap on her door, and an impish smile curved her lips. "Yes?" she called. "Who is it?"

She heard a rich chuckle. "The naked marauder."

"Oh?"

He cracked the door. "I think I left my sweatpants in there."

She presented him with her most innocent stare. "Really? What makes you think they're in here?"

He grinned devilishly. "Maybe because I got naked in there."

She pulled her lips between her teeth to keep from smiling. "In that case, Mr. Marauder, you'd better try to find them."

He ambled in, clad in his robe.

"You're not naked now," she pointed out.

He had moved to the side of the bed and could see one leg of his sweatpants protruding from beneath Billy Bob's carcass. He lifted a wry brow. "It's winter. Winter in Alaska tends to be chilly. Or hadn't you noticed?"

She smirked. "Not lately. I've had a very warm man around."

"Anybody I know?"

"You might. Good-looking." She lifted her hand to indicate height. "About so tall. Great lover."

His lips quirked. "'Fraid I don't know the guy." He indicated Billy Bob by inclining his head. "By the way, I've found my sweatpants."

She laughed, unable to hold it back any longer. "I know. You threw her out of your bed, so she had to find something of yours to sleep with. What do you plan to do about getting them?"

"Maybe bribe her with some squaw candy?"

Val shook her head, her expression purposely bland. "All gone."

His expression grew suspicious. He didn't believe a word she was saying. "What a shame."

She had an urge to run her hands through the ebony locks that fell about his shoulders. Sitting up in bed, she reminded him, "You sleep in the nude when you sleep with me. Couldn't you do that tonight?"

He was standing there lazily, his body full of indolent power, one lean hip propped on her bedpost. "Ah, but I'm not sleeping with you, remember?"

"Oh, that's right," she said, her thoughtful expression belied by the twinkle in her eyes. "Well…" She let the silence titillate him for a minute before she added, "Maybe I could help…."

White teeth flashed. "*Maybe*, nothing, sweetheart. You damned well could."

He put out a hand and she took it, sliding from between the covers. Billy Bob, who had been watching the scene with her head on her paws, lifted her snout to bare fangs in a menacing snarl.

"Fickle," Quaid told the dog.

"Jealous," Val corrected, moving beneath her man's arm. Before she left the room with Quaid, she turned back and, in a playfully confidential tone, called, "Thanks, sweetie. I owe you."

They closed the door behind them, and Quaid guided her up the steps. When they were in the shadowy loft and he was removing his robe, he asked, "I didn't think you wanted us to sleep together tonight."

She smiled lamely, feeling brazen and self-conscious. How could she ever admit that she felt like a derelict dieter, promising herself to keep away from sweets, while her greedy little mind worked at concocting a way to get at the cookie jar. It had just been her luck that Quaid had come to her door when he had, or she'd have had to make up some excuse to climb those stairs to him. Instead of confessing the whole truth, she told him, "At the time I didn't realize it was only eight-thirty. I realize, now, we have a little time to…" She sat on the bed, feeling suddenly shy and tongue-tied.

"To?" he teased.

When his robe dropped to the floor, her breathing stilled, but inside, her body hummed with heady anticipation. She could feel herself blush, and scolded, "You're shameless."

"Thanks." He inclined his head, raking her with a warm, loving gaze. "You're pretty cute yourself. I'm starting to get turned on by the mere thought of knee socks."

Laughing, she settled back against his headboard to enjoy the view. Tucking her erotically clad legs beneath her, she offered a bargain, more as a reminder to limit herself than to caution him, "One hour? Then it's off to sleep?"

"Okay," he agreed with a wolfish grin. "One hour— and a half."

She drank in the sight of his massive riveting nakedness and felt a rush of expectancy. Deep in her belly, a restless craving blossomed, and her blood grew heated. Through the haze of her lashes, she nodded her acquiescence. "But you have to promise you won't tire yourself."

His laugh was deep and resonant in the quiet night. Sprawling across the bed, he took her into his arms. With a gentle smile, he leaned forward so that his forehead rested lightly on hers, his scent rushing straight to her head. "Sweetheart, I promise I'll let you know when I'm tired."

"But you've never seemed tired.…"

He interrupted her train of thought when his hard

male lips moved against her mouth and he whispered her name with a heady mix of lust and devotion. Succumbing to her own need, Val was unable to recall what important point she'd been trying to impress upon him.

When he lifted his lips from hers, she sighed, allowing her eyelids to flutter open to gaze into his wonderful, unique face. "Quaid," she breathed, only half-teasing, "I hope one day I'll be wearing something even *more* sexy than knee socks and a big shirt when we make love...."

He teased her ear with his tongue. "In a minute you will be. Have I ever told you you have a mighty sexy birthday suit?"

"Do I?" she asked, moved by his husky compliment.

"Uh-huh..." Nipping at her jaw, her throat and then the rise of her heaving breasts, he added, "And delicious, too...."

He was true to his word. As he removed her clothes, his hand caressingly feathered her breasts, hips, the inside of her thighs. Loving his tender ministrations, she breathed his name with a reverence that made him shiver.

Val found herself clinging dreamily to him, amazed at the way he had changed her from a woman who shrank from masculine advances to the reckless, wild thing she became at his slightest glance. How she cherished this man. It was beyond her comprehension that she could love him as deeply as she did.

She moaned as his hands branded her with his ownership. Her body quivered with release, and she breathed his name through an adoring sigh. After he'd applied protection, she draped herself familiarly across his chest and smiled tentatively, drinking in the battered beauty that she'd grown to love above all else.

Her eyes devoured his potent nakedness. Unable to help herself, her fingers explored the tautness of his belly then moved down to languidly trace the fiery evidence of his passion. "I—I'm in love with you, Quaid."

He grew still. His expression was shadowed as he scanned her flushed face. "What did you say?" he whispered, the question ripe with doubt.

She couldn't help but smile at his piercingly sweet tone. "I said, I love you."

He took her exploring fingers and brought them up to his lips, kissing them before he huskily murmured, "You don't know how I've wanted to hear you say that." His lips brushing each fingertip in its turn, he asked softly, "Marry me."

She felt a thrill at his unexpected question and pulled up to better study his expression. Could he be serious?

"Oh, Quaid…" She caressed his cheek, and he pressed his lips into her palm, flecking it with his tongue before drawing her back on top of him.

"I never dreamed I'd be proposed to in exactly this way." She sighed. "But I can't think of a better position to be in…."

"No?" With a brief fiery kiss at her throat, he eased her onto her back and slid atop her. "Allow me to show you a few *very* interesting positions—since we only have an hour and a half."

Giddy laughter bubbled from her throat. "You're crazy, you know?"

"I climb ice."

"Among other things," she uttered suggestively, curling her arms about his neck.

He smiled down at her and then kissed her slightly parted lips, murmuring, "That was a yes, wasn't it?"

"Yes—yes—yes," she cried, her heart so full that she couldn't hold back her joyous tears.

With exquisite gentleness, he slipped inside her. Settled together, touching deeply and completely, he had to swallow a tremor of emotion before he could add, "I do love you, Val. So much, it hurts." The declaration came out rough yet poignantly tender.

With the thrill of their blissful connection and Quaid's unexpected vow, flames of desire leaped high within Val. The stimulating movements of his body made her gasp.

Lowering his face to hers, he dropped feather-light kisses along her jaw. "I'm a damn lucky bastard," he muttered brokenly, his eyes stinging with gratitude. Then, somehow renewed, he lifted himself upward until they were almost separated. In a potent yet tempered thrust, he drew from her a throaty sigh. Lowering his lips to hers, he vowed in a low, passion-drenched voice, "And I will love you, Val—tonight—always. Don't ever doubt that."

Quaid guided her, thrusting in a slow yet ever-building tempo. Val, her body thrilling, arched against him, driven by his whispered promise as much as the heightened feelings he was eliciting within her. Their mingled moans of pleasure became a melodious beginning for this special night of loving.

13

THE KITCHEN, golden and cozy, was a warm haven in the early-morning darkness. Quaid and Val sat without speaking, each shut away within their own thoughts. Val looked apprehensively at the kitchen clock. 6:46 a.m. Only two minutes had passed since the last time she'd peered at it. She took another bite of her scrambled eggs, not tasting them. How was she going to make it through this day when every minute seemed like a week—and Quaid wasn't even out of her sight, yet!

Her deflated sigh lifted Quaid's gaze. "You okay?"

She forced a smile. "Sure." Pushing herself up, she fairly dashed to the refrigerator, hoping movement would calm her jangled nerves. "Want any more orange juice?"

He declined with a shake of his head. "I'm fine." Billy Bob, lying at Quaid's side, looked up, sensing tension. Quaid patted her big head, murmuring something soothing that Val couldn't make out.

As she watched him calming the dog, she stilled the refrigerator door gaping in her grasp. Her gaze trailed over the man sitting at her little kitchen table. He appeared outwardly composed, but she had been through too much with him not to know that inside he was in turmoil. Still, the time for talking about it was past, and she kept her concerns to herself.

Her eyes lingered hungrily on him, yet with great regret. This must be how women all over the world, in every age of history, had felt when their men were about to go off to do battle, not knowing if they'd see their men whole again. She bit the inside of her cheek. Shame on her! He'd be back tonight—happy, tired and victorious. *Of course he would.* Some dark part of her brain nagged doggedly that somehow the climb would go terribly awry. Why wasn't the world different? Why couldn't she just tell him not to go and have him blindly obey her? But, she reminded herself, what kind of a man would he be then? Certainly not the one she'd fallen in love with.

Quaid was wearing a hunter-green turtleneck sweater. His wide shoulders seemed to dwarf the battered old table. He was unquestionably an imposing, capable man. *He'll be fine,* she told herself. If anyone in the world could beat Death Scream, Quaid Perrault could.

"Are you hot?" he queried, one brow lifting in question.

She jumped at the sound of his voice. "What?"

He indicated the refrigerator door, yawning open. "Since the orange juice is in front, I figured you must be after the cool air. It'd be cheaper to walk outside if you're overheated."

Trying to cast off her forebodings, she threw him a mischievous look. "And when did you come up with *that* cure for overheatedness. Last night, you never mentioned anything about me walking outside when I was…overheated."

He rested his chin on his knuckles and cocked a knowing half grin. "Sweetheart, I have a great affection for the environment. And considering your state last night, had you gone outside, Valdez Glacier would have melted, and half the continental United States would be underwater today."

She threw him a skeptical smirk and walked over to stroke his freshly shaved jaw. "Quite the concerned environmentalist, aren't you?" she murmured, kissing his temple. "But just whose fault is it that I was, shall we say, febrile, last night."

He looked at her askance. "Febrile?"

Sliding her arms about his shoulders to rest them on his chest, she said, "I read a lot."

"That's not all you do." He took her hands into his and drew her fingers to his lips. "Febrile, huh?" he repeated thoughtfully. "Okay. If febrile means sexy, loving and inventive in bed, I'll buy it."

She laughed at him. "It means nothing of the sort, Mr. College Man, and you know it."

He stood and turned to face her. "I know what I like." With his teeth nipping her lips, he murmured, "Just on the off chance I don't know what it means—" he patted her tempting derriere "—do you want to go...look it up?"

Quaid's voice held a seductive message that had nothing to do with improving their minds.

His coffee-laced breath heated her skin; his tempting words, her heart. But she knew time was short and that he had to meet Ross in the canyon in thirty minutes. He knew it, too, and was only teasing her. Trying for lightheartedness, she quipped, "I'm not the greatest housekeeper in the world. It might take me a while to find the dictionary."

"Could you find it by tonight?"

"Probably."

"Good." Pressing her hips into his, he let her know very graphically that she was a tremendous turn-on for him, even clad in her lead-gray sweats.

She felt herself blush, and he kissed her pinkened cheek. "Now, that's the cutest example of febricity I've ever witnessed." He grinned lovingly, taking her burning cheeks between his cool hands. For a heartbeat he merely looked at her, his gaze lingering, filled with sweet longing.

He kissed her firmly and possessively, and just when Val was about to forsake her promise to herself that she *not* beg him to stay, he pulled reluctantly away. His features suddenly solemn, he reminded her, "I'd better get ready."

She stiffened, her chest constricting with apprehension. She'd been trying not to think about this moment, trying not to watch the clock ticking the minutes away, trying not to face the fact that Quaid's life would be put at risk today. She swallowed, only to find that her throat was prickly dry. With nothing left for them to say, she acknowledged the truth with a diffident nod.

Averting her gaze, she mumbled, "I—I'll go warm up the VW."

"Thanks."

He started to kiss her once again, but she stepped away, retreating from his encompassing warmth. She'd made it halfway to the front door when she turned back. "Oh—I forgot. My mechanic said your Jeep's ready any time."

He half turned, nodded and then started up the steps before she once again halted him, calling, "Quaid—I'm going to volunteer to be on call for rescue duty. After I drop you off, I'll go out to the hangar and give the state troopers a call."

He turned fully around. Frowning, he curled his fingers over the railing. "Don't you want to watch?"

She smiled at him, but there was no happiness in it. "I don't think I could stand it. I can keep busy at the hangar. Slim and Mazie will be there. We'll do some spring cleaning. Time will pass better."

"Spring cleaning? In February?"

She reached for her coat. "We're not shackled to tradition at Sourdough WhirlyTours. We do spring cleaning whenever we're all in the office, and I'm either without work or hyper."

Sardonic amusement altered his expression. "Oh, then they don't know it's spring cleaning day, yet."

"It's usually best to keep it a surprise."

"I'd hoped you'd..." He smiled morosely. "Are you sure you don't want to be in the canyon?"

She nodded.

His long, accepting sigh filled the silence. Shrugging his hands into his pockets, he murmured, "Do what you have to do, darling."

They stared at each other. Val's eyes telegraphed the message that she knew that today he, too, would be doing something he had to do, and there wasn't a thing she could say to change his mind. She cast her gaze down to mask her misgivings. Seconds later, she'd disappeared into the moonlit predawn—an eerie mural of bright crusted snow and goblinish shadows.

ROSS HAD BEEN WAITING for them when Val's decrepit VW bus pulled up alongside the highway. He ran toward the bus, scattering clods of snow. His wiry body was outlined in the glare of the headlights, the orange wind suit he wore looking bloodred in the glare. Swinging his pack to his shoulder, he shouted, "Hi, partners. Are we ready to take on this big dumb devil in shining armor?"

With a shove on the jammed passenger door, Quaid popped it open and climbed down, dragging his pack from the back. As he did so, Ross ambled around to

Val's door and motioned for her to roll down the window. "Hi, beautiful. All set to make history?"

She reached out of the window and patted Ross's cold cheek. "Actually, I'm all set for you and Quaid to come over for dinner tonight to celebrate your victory. I plan to whip up some goat stir-fry just the way you like it. You finish the climb by five. Dinner will be ready by six."

Ross's expression closed in confusion. "Aren't you going with us?"

She shifted her gaze to Quaid, who'd rounded the VW to stand beside Ross. Keeping her eyes on the tall man with the somber, scarred face, she said, "I'm not ready to tackle Death Scream yet, Ross. You two soften it up for me, okay?"

He shifted his gaze from her face to Quaid's. "Seriously?"

Quaid nodded. "Seriously." Leaning down, he brushed Val's lips with one last kiss. Before he drew away, he murmured, "For luck."

The nervous tension she detected in those two words made her wince. Slipping her hands to his face, she drew his lips against hers again and vowed softly, "Forever."

They lingered there, cheek to cheek for another precious second before he pulled back. Without glancing toward Ross, he headed out across the canyon, barking, "Come on, old man. Time's wasting." The morning crust atop the frozen snow broke under his climbing boots as he trudged away, the squeaky crunch growing rapidly distant.

"Well, well…" Ross intoned, drawing Val's gaze. He shook his head at her and smiled wryly. "Well, well, well…" With that, he lifted a jaunty salute and affirmed quietly, "Wish it'd been me, but since it couldn't be, I'm glad it was that one-eyed donkey's rear."

"*Ross?* You coming?" Quaid shouted.

The older man waved over his shoulder. "I'm coming, I'm coming. Just saying goodbye to my favorite lady." He winked at Val, grumbling good-naturedly, "He's a lucky bum."

She reached out and squeezed Ross's arm. "I love you, too."

"Yeah." His smile was wan. "I make a great brother."

"Be careful."

"Count on it. There's some lady out there who'd be real sad if I bought the farm before I found her and made her life a living hell."

She laughed despite her nervousness. "The only way you could make a woman's life a living hell would be to take your friendship away from her."

He tweaked her cheek. "Then your life will never be a living hell, Val."

She was touched, and the shimmer in her eyes showed it. "Now go on. And don't be late for dinner."

"For one of your dinners? Only over my…" They both heard the unspoken implication. Ross shrugged it off. "See ya, pretty lady."

With that he tugged his pack more securely over his shoulder and jogged after Quaid, yelling, "Say, Perrault! Did I tell you about my night blindness? Maybe you'd better lead the first pitch."

Off in the distance, she could hear Quaid laugh at Ross's joke. The sound was strong and rich, like his coffee, his grin and his lovemaking. She couldn't see him very well. Just vaguely, where his black wind suit blotted out the faint gleam of ice at the terminus of Death

Scream, but she knew he'd be putting on his climbing harness and crampons by this time.

Turning away from Ross's receding figure, she looked around. A crowd had begun to drift into the canyon, mostly well-wishers, a few morbidly curious. In an hour the canyon would be jammed with spectators. Though there would be other climbers there going up other routes, Death Scream was the big news around Valdez, its danger was well documented.

She saw Sam Marling, a close friend and the state trooper in charge of coordinating rescue operations for the festival, if any were needed. Sam cruised slowly by, and she waved. When he waved back, she pulled onto the highway, her studded tire grabbing at the icy glaze as she headed off toward her chopper's hangar to sweat out the day.

QUAID PULLED A LENGTH of rope from his pack and tied in. When Ross was ready, they donned headlamps that would assist them in the first hour of the climb, before daylight came to Keystone Canyon.

They'd decided that Quaid would lead the first, third and final pitch, while Ross would lead the second and "killer" fourth. So Quaid started up first. Above him he could see ice dimly glinting. Behind him, there was nothing but blackness, broken only by a few meandering flashlight beams. The canyon was blocked from the moon's direct illumination by high cliffs.

In the early-morning darkness, their strength fully intact and their toes and fingers still warm, the climb went smoothly. Wind was out of the north and steady at ten knots, with the temperature around twenty-five. All in all, conditions were near ideal.

As dawn began to break, Quaid could make out colors in the ice-blues and greens glittering in the towering monolith above him, and the outline of ragged cliffs became visible in the southeast quadrant of the canyon where the sky was turning a pale gray. Forty minutes later, the gray was tempering into blue, but the sun would never shine directly into the canyon—not in February. Only when they reached the lofty rim of Death Scream would they see the sun. Swinging his Zero, a state-of-the-art ice tool, in a powerful arc above his head, Quaid moved doggedly toward his objective.

After two hours, his adrenaline was still revved to high gear and his mind was totally focused. He was amazed by his mental state, elevated to a level that was hard to describe. He was exactly where he needed to be—honed to a supersensitive edge. His nerves were calm, and he knew that, with his consciousness quickened to such a totally alert plane, he would make no mistakes.

The noon hour came as Quaid and Ross stopped at a resting point or belay stance, each anchored to two ice screws, where they broke out lunch before beginning the third pitch.

The ascent was arduous, draining both of them measurably. Nevertheless, by two o'clock, both climbers had successfully reached the overhang of ice that represented the beginning of the fourth pitch. Ross had won the toss, giving him the honor and burden of being at the sharp end of the rope on this, the most difficult portion of the climb. It consisted of a full fifty-meter freestanding ribbon of ice separated from rock by twenty feet, with no place to plant protection between belay stances.

Ross seemed pale. To complicate things, the wind had picked up to nearly forty knots, tossing their ropes and sending snow spinning into their faces and down their necks. This new, feisty blow had been howling and whining around them for a quarter of an hour, making communication difficult. Now that they were resting together, Quaid asked, "You okay?"

Ross took a slug of water from his thermos and grinned at his friend. "What's the matter, you getting tired?"

"I'm dragging," Quaid admitted. "We could do with less wind."

Ross grunted in agreement. "My mama didn't tell me there'd be days like this."

"Your mama didn't know you were such an idiot."

"Look who's talkin', ol' buddy," Ross wisecracked. "You've been up here before."

Quaid glanced down. The crowd below had swollen, jamming the canyon with very chilly spectators, and traffic was gridlocked on the highway. Shaking his head, he looked at Ross. "I didn't get this high last time. You remember that overhanging snow cornice on the third pitch?"

Ross rolled his eyes. "A real sweat breaker."

"That's where I lost it last time—in some loose ice."

Ross laughed, appearing his old self again. "I couldn't tell, man. Congratulations." He held out a gloved hand.

Quaid took it. "Thanks. Now, what do you say we attack this killer pitch." He swatted Ross's back. "And don't crack that damned icicle. I don't feel like being attached to a falling Ross, attached to a thousand-ton ice bullet."

"Gotcha." Ross swung out onto the overhanging icicle, cranked off a pull-up and began to front-point gingerly upward. With every swing of his ax, the pillar gave off a nerve-racking "thunk," reminding them that Ross was attempting to scale something that was very unstable. Like a diamond being cut, the wrong move could shatter it—and send anyone climbing its jagged surface spiraling into nothingness.

Quaid noticed that the configuration of the undulating ice was causing Ross a center-of-gravity problem. As Ross reached upward he was forced to lean way over to his right to follow the sturdiest ice. He had to be careful not to cant too far away from his center of gravity, or his crampons would pop free.

Quaid had just fed Ross some rope, when Ross's crampons did just what Quaid had been fearing. They pulled free from the ice, and Ross let out a frightened yelp, arcing wildly outward, his legs flailing as he hung on for dear life to one lone ice tool.

Quaid froze, gripping the rope to take the shock in the event that Ross fell. Luckily Ross regained himself and was momentarily moving up the face, undaunted. With a flippant shout over his shoulder, he made light of the situation with, "We gotta make it *look* hard, ol' buddy. Don't want the folks down below to get bored."

Quaid blew a sigh through his teeth and relaxed his rigid muscles, feeding Ross additional rope. Some minutes later, when Ross was about halfway to his next belay stance, Quaid heard it: an ominous grinding and creaking far above his head.

"*Ohhhh,* daaaaaamn!" Ross cried. "*It's coming down, man!*"

Quaid ground out a prayer for them both as he watched his buddy frantically scramble to his left, clawing with his axes for any miserly purchase on the ice. Quaid could see the pillar shudder and he cursed, a surge of desperate alarm ripping through him. In another minute, they both could be crushed by tons of falling ice. It could be all over for them in a matter of seconds. He closed his eyes as he thought of Val, of what they might have had—

A harsh roar caught his attention, and his gaze shot up to become riveted on a huge chunk of ice that had broken away from the pillar where Ross had perched only seconds before. It plummeted toward Quaid like a meteor sprung from some distant death star.

He could do little to escape it, knotted to three screws as he was, except flatten himself to the ice. By some miracle, that was enough to allow the hurtling projectile to thunder past with a sickening sucking noise.

He heard the cries from below and saw people scurrying and diving for safety. He could only stare in horror, powerless to help. After what seemed like an hour but what must have only been seconds, it was clear that everyone on the ground had made it to safety. Quaid looked up to see Ross hanging precariously, one foot jabbing at rotting ice for a toehold.

Quaid felt sweat trickle down his back, though the wind was cold and snow was blowing all around him. Stark panic was building in his gut. Would they be next to go screaming toward the earth? Fighting his fear, he'd started to call out something encouraging, when one of Ross's ice axes pulled and he screamed, "*Hell*— I'm *losing*—" The wind caught part of what he'd said and carried it away into oblivion, but his meaning was all too clear. Ross believed he was going to fall.

"Hang in there, man!" Quaid shouted back, bracing to stop his friend's descent if, indeed, Ross really was losing it.

With a string of enraged curses, Ross peeled away from the weakened ice column, tumbling toward Quaid with a macabre sort of grace. As he spun by,

Ross stretched his arms toward his friend in a futile gesture of supplication, his ice axes, rotating with deadly force at the end of his wrist loops. Quaid saw Ross's eyes—angry, vulnerable—and he knew that look would be burned in his brain for the rest of his life, which might not be very long. *"Damn it to hell!"* he ground out. Ross wasn't going to crater if *he* had anything to say about it. Neither of them were!

Even protected, three ice screws holding them solidly at the belay point, Quaid was dismayed to hear the ugly "ping" of a screw being yanked from the ice by the force of Ross's descent. Though tensed and prepared for the shock, when it came, it lifted Quaid off his stance, slamming his shoulder into the unforgiving ice. Jouncing around, his expression tight with pain, Quaid mouthed a prayer that the other two screws would hold.

Ross fell away until the rope finally caught him up, bouncing him about like a big baggy yo-yo in the hands of an inept King Kong. A huge moan went up from the canyon floor, and then utter, deafening silence.

Quaid cringed as he watched, recalling the misery of being yanked by his own back rope the last time he'd attempted Death Scream. But unlike theirs today, his had failed him, allowing him to fall the remaining distance to the feet of the horrified spectators below.

As soon as he could, Quaid hammered in a screw to replace the one that had been yanked loose. When he had the third screw set, he cast a fearful glance down to see Ross dangling in a slow spin and called, "Talk to me, man! You okay? Do you want to rap down?"

Ross squinted up into the wind-whipped snow. Taking up the axes that dangled from his wrist loops, he swung an arm, attaching himself to the frozen cascade.

"Negative. I'm okay." He sounded a little winded. "Just got a couple of bruised ribs."

The wind had died enough for his shout to be heard on the ground, and a rousing cheer rose up to boost their spirits. Ross, with amazing bravado considering what he'd just been through, waved an ax at them, shouting, "That's why we get paid the big bucks!"

He looked up at Quaid, calling less loudly, "You want the honor of lead hog, man?" He winked. "I'll give it up if you beg."

Relaxing a bit, Quaid shook his head at his scrappy friend. "After we get your rear up here, I'll go take a look."

Ross laughed. "Thought you might."

They surged forward without any further problem, except for the fact that Ross seemed to be very fatigued, though he refused to admit it. His breathing was hard, his complexion bordered on gray, but his smile was bright and his attitude salty. Quaid knew there would be no convincing Ross to halt the climb, short of bashing him in the head and rendering him unconscious. So Quaid kept his mouth shut and climbed, hoping he was overreacting.

It was nearly four o'clock and Quaid was within forty feet of the rim of the canyon when Ross quit feeding him rope. Caught there on a candlesticked overhang of ice, Quaid turned to peer down at his buddy. "What's with you, Rosco? I'm stuck up here like a dog on a leash."

Ross was hunched in his harness at the last belay point, his head lolling forward.

"Ross?" Quaid called over the howling wind and blowing snow. "Hey, man. What's the matter?"

With great effort Ross rolled his head back and blinked upward. Quaid was shocked to see his face, ghastly, ashen and distorted by pain. Ross croaked something unintelligible. The only word Quaid could hear was, "heart…" With that, Ross caved in and hung there like a cast-off puppet.

Quaid stared at the inert body of his best friend, his lips opening in dumb shock. After a few seconds, the seriousness of their predicament seeped in, and something hot and electric shot through Quaid—something very like terror. He cast his gaze around him. What the hell was he going to do? He couldn't climb down. Like cat's claws, crampons were built for going up, not down. And with Ross unconscious, he couldn't feed out any rope for Quaid to use for climbing. Neither were there any descent anchors for him to use to rappel down to his friend.

Quaid jerked his head to the left. He was out about thirty feet from the rock face with one hundred meters of sky between him and the nearest cliff. He had to twist his head far to the right to check it out, since that was his blind side. There was nothing hopeful over there, either. Nothing but more damned sky. *Hell.* He wished he had wings!

Wings? He blinked dumbly at the pocked ice inches from his face. How could he have been so stupid? Wasted so much time? Val—she had wings.

Belatedly finding his wits, he yelled down, hoping for a lull in the wind to carry his message to the crowd below. "Get a chopper. Heart attack!" He repeated the cry until he saw scurrying among the watchers and then a clot of people running toward the canyon's mouth to flag down Sam, the state trooper on duty.

Quaid shifted, looking back at Ross, who hadn't moved. What was he going to do? He could put in a couple of shaky ice screws and wait to be rescued, but Quaid feared that Ross couldn't hold out that long. His friend needed help now, and there wasn't anybody up there to help him but Quaid.

Hanging by his Zeros, Quaid's crampons were stuck in little steps he'd kicked in the rotten ice. His arms were burning unmercifully, and he was tremendously tired. Just hanging there was a grueling effort after eight hours of dragging himself up this grudging slice of hell. But he had to try something. He couldn't just let Ross dangle there and die.

He squinted up into the swirling snow. Forty feet above him loomed the pinnacle of Death Scream. He could see the sun glinting off the topmost ice. So near and yet...

The only way to help Ross was to climb up there. He'd have to untie from the rope and finish the climb *free-soloing.* He'd be totally unprotected, but it was the only way. Once he reached the top he could "post-hole"—scramble via soft, knee-deep snow—the hundred yards to a gully, where he'd down-climb through steep snow and stunted alders. Then, still unprotected, Quaid would have to inch laterally out over a thin smear of ice to his buddy. That way, when the helicopter came, he'd have Ross ready to be airlifted to the hospital. If he didn't try it, the time lost could prove fatal.

All it would take was a little damned courage. His mind battled with his body, the humanitarian side of him trying to force his reticent, shivering limbs to move. "You only have forty feet to go," he told himself grimly. *"Forty lousy feet!"*

He squeezed his fists around his ice tools, his hands already so frozen he could barely hold on anymore. Focusing on the top of the pillar, he mumbled, "Up—dammit!" Then he growled it. "Up—*up!*" Finally, his voice breaking, he shouted it, tears blurring his objective, "Go *up*, Perrault. Untie, and move your butt up there. *It's only forty goddamn feet!*"

Costly seconds ticked by. Still Quaid couldn't quite block out the loathsome inner voice that jeered, *But if you make one small mistake, you have 960 feet to fall.*

14

"GOOD GRIEF," Val grumbled. Her eyes were at floor level as she crouched on her knees between the filing cabinet and the all-purpose shelves that Mazie referred to jokingly as never-never land. Val called over her shoulder, "I didn't find the box of paper clips, but this place is crammed full of disgusting dust balls. Ugh. How long has it been since we cleaned under here?"

"What year is this?" Mazie sat down in the swivel chair beside the crackling VHF radio and mopped her smudged brow. "And don't call 'em dust balls, boss. Do what my kids do."

Val crawled backward out of the narrow dusty space and frowned up at her secretary. "I'm afraid to ask what your kids do, Mazie."

The older woman took a sip of her cola. "It's not so bad. They just call 'em dust gerbils. They name 'em and keep 'em as pets—beats cleaning under their beds."

Val shook her head at her secretary. "Mazie, you really must write a book about child rearing one day. But for now, let's indulge an idiosyncrasy of mine and get rid of the dust gerbils."

"Well, okay." Mazie shrugged, looking doubtful. Pushing her sweater sleeves back up to her elbows, she lumbered from her chair. "But, you realize they would never have discovered penicillin if they'd been as picky about a little dirt as you're being."

Val's nerves had been wound tight all day in her

anxiety over Quaid and Ross, but she'd been keeping a close eye on the time. Only one hour more and the men would be safely to the top of Death Scream. Beginning to feel as though her fears had been unfounded, she sat back on her heels and allowed herself to laugh. "I wouldn't call cleaning out from under the filing cabinet once a year all that picky."

Mazie planted her hands on her hips, looking around distractedly. "Where's the broom?"

"Slim may have it. I'll go check." Swiping at the dust on her sweatpants, she headed out of the overheated, dusty office into the chill of the hangar to find Slim sorting through oily rags.

"Slim. We've lost the broom again. Any ideas where it might be this time?"

"Did you check the stack of stuff we set out for the Goodwill? That'd be Mazie's idea of a good place for it." He straightened up, peering at her. His walrus mustache lifted in a grin. "Did you know you have a smudge right across your nose?" he queried with a chuckle.

"Oh?" She grimaced, holding out a hand. "Can I have a rag?"

He seemed to consider a couple, trying to decide which was less filthy. "I don't know, Val. You use one of these, ya might end up with a face that could lubricate a rotor head—"

"Boss! *Boss!*" Mazie came running out into the hangar, her sweater flapping open in the cold. "Just got a call from the troopers. There's an emergency situation at Keystone Canyon."

Val spun around, her heart stopping. "What is it?"

Mazie caught her breath, her fingers splayed over her heaving bosom. "They didn't know for sure. Just said to get a chopper over there."

"Okay—" Val ran for her coveralls, almost colliding

with Slim, who'd already scooped them up. He all but threw them in her face, shouting, "I'll get the hangar door and drive the bus outside. You just get in that ship!"

In the winter, because of the difficulty of moving a helicopter across glazed ice, Val kept her chopper on a trailer. This morning, after she'd arrived, she'd attached the trailer to the bumper hitch on her VW bus in preparation for just such an emergency.

By the time she was settled behind the controls of her lemon-yellow Jet Ranger, Slim was driving the van out onto the ice. The VW's studded tires struggled to pull the heavy burden of both trailer and chopper clear of the hangar.

All the while, Val's heart was hammering in her chest and blocking her throat, making breathing difficult. She noticed her hands were trembling and her palms were damp as she yanked on her gloves. She was hard-pressed to keep from dropping into a hysterical heap and screaming and sobbing, *"I knew it! I knew this would happen!"* Just as she'd feared, something had gone terribly wrong on Death Scream.

All she could see was Quaid, lying at its base, broken and—

God! It was after four. If they'd fallen so late in the day, there would be no hope for survival. Still, Sam had called for a chopper. He wouldn't have done that if there'd been no hope. Would he?

Slim pounded on her door to let her know that everything was clear and she could take off. Biting back her gnawing terror, she gave him a grim thumbs-up, started the engine and twisted the throttle on full.

Rising the collective with her left hand, the Jet Ranger lifted off and she headed toward Keystone Canyon. While the outskirts of Valdez sped by beneath her, her mind screamed, *Why does it seem like I'm stand-*

*ing still? Why does air travel seem so unforgivably slow all
of a sudden?*

In what seemed like days, weeks, eons, but had, in
reality, only taken seven minutes, she was circling
above the canyon, preparing to settle to the gorge's
floor. Unable to help herself, she scanned Death
Scream, and what she saw made cold dread spread
through her body. One lone climber—clad in orange—
remained on the ice face. *One man.* She blinked, disbelieving, her worst nightmare confirmed. Quaid was
gone.

A tear trailed down her cheek, and she had to rein in
a surge of hysterical, blind rage in order to maneuver
her rescue craft into the canyon below. The wind
whipped and bucked her helicopter, and she forced
herself to concentrate on her job. The gale that fun-
neled through the canyon was strong enough to slam
her into a rock wall where she and her ship would be
reduced to a fiery shower of debris above the cowering
crowd. Though she felt dead inside, she knew that if,
by some miracle, there was a spark of life left in Quaid
Perrault's body, she could not allow a foolish fatal er-
ror to destroy his chances for survival. So she had to
live, had to do her job.

Lowering the collective, she settled to the canyon
floor, scattering snow and chasing away spectators.
Sam, the trooper who'd waved to her that morning,
came running up, crouched and holding on to his fur
hat with both hands. She frictioned the controls down
and was climbing out when Sam reached her.

"Where is he?" Not even trying to mask her anguish,
she shouted the question over the pulsating din created by the spinning rotor.

"Up there." Sam cocked his head toward Death
Scream.

She followed his gaze, confused. "No. I mean the—victim."

Sam squinted at her. "That *is* the victim. Looks like a heart attack. You're going to have to get them off the ice, Val."

"Them?" she yelled. "There's only one man up there."

"The other guy's—" He pointed. "See, there he is, coming out of the brush onto the ice. A few minutes more, and they'll be ready to haul ass to the hospital."

"Coming out of the—" She spun around to stare upward, and her eyes widened in a mixture of shock and utter relief as she watched the distant figure—*in a black windsuit*—inching sideways toward the unmoving orange body.

Feeling a rush of new panic, she realized Quaid was nine hundred feet above the ground without protection. "How did he get there?" she shouted, wiping her blowing hair from her face.

Sam shook his head. "Damnedest thing. For a couple of minutes after he yelled for help, he just sat there. If it'd been me, I'da been making my peace with the Almighty. Whatever—he finally untied his rope and *dogged* if he didn't climb on up and over the top." Letting go of his hat with one hand, Sam motioned broadly to his left, shouting, "Then he scrambled along that cliff there and climbed down."

"But—" She twisted around to stare at Sam. "He free-soloed? Up *there?*" She almost choked on her own heart, knowing he must have fought a mighty internal battle to find the courage to do that.

"Is that what you call it?" He shrugged. "Whatever, it was the gamest piece of work I've ever seen. When that guy went over the top, the canyon went wild. I never heard so much yellin' in my life. You'd a thought we'd won a war or something."

"Maybe somebody did...." She sighed under her breath, her lips trembling. Wiping the back of her gloves across her misty eyes, she berated herself. This was no time to break down. They weren't safe yet, not by a long shot.

Quaid, still free-soloing so horribly far above the canyon floor, had almost reached Ross, and Val knew it was time for her to go. "Okay, Sam, I need a weight for my rescue line. Anything that's heavy. What can you get me?"

The trooper looked around, losing his hat to the rotor's wind. "Damn! Say—" He jerked a fist in the air as though he'd just caught an idea. "Would a wine bota do? My cousin Harry's got one right over there." He pointed into the hovering crowd, their faces turned upward, expectant, worried, as they watched the drama play out before them.

Val took off a glove and wiped a damp palm on her coveralls. She'd never had an emergency where someone had to be pulled off the ice. With this wind, the rescue would be tricky. Swallowing, she darted a glance back up to gauge Quaid's progress. The pressure of time crowded in on her. "Get the bota, Sam. It'll have to do."

By the time Sam got back with the half-filled goatskin bag, Val had the rescue line ready. While she climbed into her ship, Sam attached the bota and, in a low crouch, dashed away while she lifted off and circled toward Death Scream. The wind was rushing through the canyon, and she delicately worked the controls to compensate, climbing away as quickly as she could manage.

Suddenly there they were—one hundred yards straight ahead. Quaid was spread-eagled around Ross, but upon hearing her approach, he turned and waved.

And then to her absolute amazement, he threw her a kiss.

With one hand on the collective and the other on the cyclic, she couldn't respond in kind, but her heart answered with a missed beat, and her whole body grew warm, grateful that he was safe.

Lifting away, she cut around until she was directly above them, maneuvering the line with the bouncing bota into place. It was tedious and exacting work in the best conditions, but fighting forty-knot winds in dwindling daylight, bordered on feeblemindedness. She decided to be like Scarlett O'Hara, and just not think about it right now.

Inwardly she prayed that Quaid would still have the strength and coordination to get them connected on the first try. Not only did every second count for Ross, but the day was fading. In about thirty minutes Valdez would be trussed up in darkness, and there was no moon. They had only minutes to get this right.

QUAID HAD SEEN VAL circle into the canyon and had never known such happiness in his life. It was a damned shame that he had neither the strength nor the time to let out a yelp of laughter. As her chopper had settled into the canyon, he'd bent to his work, thrashing through a dense growth of devil's club. He had yet to reach Ross, and his right arm felt as though it would come off at any second. His fingers were long past tired and were frozen and clumsy as his body functioned on pure desperation.

When he reached Ross and tied into the screws he'd placed over an hour ago, Quaid tugged off a glove with his teeth and checked his friend's pulse. He could detect nothing in his wrist and moved quickly to check the carotid artery in his throat. A pulse was there—but too fast. Much too fast. He leaned near Ross's mouth, was able to hear faint panting sounds and breathed a sigh of relief. There was still time.

It surprised him when Ross opened his eyes and grinned weakly. "You bring the pizza I ordered?"

Sliding stiffened fingers back into his glove, he cautioned, "Maybe you'd better save the jokes for a while." Quaid was surprised at his voice, weak and hoarse with stress.

Ross closed his eyes. "Sorry, man. Thought I could handle it with medication…"

"Shut up. We'll talk tomorrow."

"Hey—" Ross's eyes fluttered opened. "How'd you get here?"

"Just passing by. Be quiet. Val is coming."

"She's a good kid."

"She's starting to make a habit out of saving my life."

Ross's lips quirked in a small, pained smile, but he didn't say anything more.

Just then, the weighted line danced to within ten feet of them. Quaid grabbed for it but missed. *"Damn,"* he spat, but couldn't hear it for the booming pulse of the chopper's rotor overhead.

The rescue line twirled in their direction again. Fighting the down draft from the chopper blades and the cyclone of snow it had dislodged, Quaid nabbed the dancing rope with the serrated edge of his ice ax. Very cautiously he drew it in. Though his fingers were deadened and awkward, he managed to hook Ross's climbing harness to the line. Then, his strength ebbing near zero, he did the same with his own before dragging out his Swiss army knife and cutting them loose from their belay point.

Immediately and with a frightening lurch downward, they swung away from the cliff face and then, with a sharp wallop on one of Quaid's dangling legs, rammed back into it. The chopper had been dragged down several feet as it took their weight, and Quaid's stomach bounced into his throat. He'd been trying to support Ross's lolling head, but he grabbed onto the line with one flailing arm as the wind caught them and whipped them in a wide arc.

Sailing through the air at seventy miles an hour, completely unprotected from the elements, was not an experience Quaid had dreamed of having. Now, yanked around in space, snow and freezing air biting his face, he decided it was an experience he didn't plan to endure again.

Ross moaned and shivered, and Quaid did his best to protect his friend from the punishment of the elements by crouching over him.

They spun crazily around and around, battered to and fro. Val knew their ride was rough, and she wished there had been another way. But there wasn't. This was the fastest rescue method available. So she kept an eye on them via the rearview mirror, located near her feet and turned downward through the glass bubble. Mouthing a prayer for them, she set a direct course for the hospital.

Quaid's arms ached from his tensed position and he gritted his teeth to keep from yelling at the top of his lungs that he'd had just about all he could stand, when suddenly he realized they were settling gently above a big round helipad located in the hospital parking lot. There was quite a bit of activity below them. He could see white-coated hospital personnel, a couple of stretchers and various pieces of equipment he didn't recognize.

Minutes later, Ross's motionless form had been wheeled into the hospital. Quaid was standing on the ground, refusing a stretcher, struggling through a batch of reporters to get to Val as she climbed down from her chopper.

She ran into his arms, and she felt unbelievably good, smelling of oil and dust and faintly of lily of the valley. He'd never smelled anything so wonderful in his life. Sweeping her into his arms, he was surprised to find that she was very light and that he felt absolutely no fatigue. "Val. Am I glad to see you," he breathed, his voice cracking with tension.

"Me, too." She kissed his cheek, his jaw, his throat. "You must be exhausted."

"I should be, shouldn't I?" he chuckled, his breath ruffling her hair.

Stepping back, she took his hand. He looked so wonderful, even with his face windburned and nicked from devil's club and falling shards of ice. "Let's go inside so they can see to those cuts. How's Ross?"

Quaid shook his head. "I don't know. He's alive. The doctor's with him."

"He'll be all right," Val stated grimly, her expression determined.

"Yeah," Quaid agreed, squeezing her fingers reassuringly. "He's held on this long. He'll make it."

An apprehensive silence descended over them as they headed inside to wait for news. With her hand in his, Quaid limped along beside her. Noting the infirmity, Val turned toward him, her brow creasing. "You're hurt."

He shook his head. "Just a little goodbye kiss Death Scream gave me."

"Damn wind," she muttered. At her insistence, he slung an arm about her shoulder so that she could help support him. Hugging him to her as they walked, she whispered, "You'll be okay."

He squeezed her shoulders, lovingly. "Sweetheart, I

was okay the minute I saw my little knight and her lemon-yellow charger heading my way."

VAL WAS JOLTED AWAKE, muddled and confused, wondering why she was sleeping sitting up. Glancing down, she noticed Quaid's head, his left cheek freshly bandaged, was nestled in her lap. When she'd jerked awake, so had he. As he sat up, Val belatedly looked up to see the woman in surgical greens who'd awakened her with a touch on her shoulder.

The woman, her eyes red from crying, asked quietly, "Mrs. Knox?"

"No…" Feeling suddenly apprehensive, Val shot to her feet. "Mrs. Knox died six years ago. I'm—" She indicated Quaid, who'd also risen to his feet. "We're friends of Ross's."

The woman sniffled into a handkerchief. "Oh—well, hello, I'm Dr. Morty—Sondra Morty." She held out a hand.

Val stared blankly, ignoring polite niceties. "What's wrong? Is Ross—" Her voice caught, and tears came to her eyes. "He's not dead!"

"What?" The doctor looked stung. "Why, no. He's going to be fine. Ross has a condition called paroxysmal atrial tachycardia. As I understand it, he's been handling it with medication. But the strain of climbing today was too much for him." She paused to dab at her eyes. "He's always been such a proud, stubborn fool."

"You know Ross?" Quaid asked quietly.

"I'm an old school friend. I just moved back to Valdez last month, and wouldn't you know the first week I'm on call for the ER, he comes in all pale and weak—" She broke off to delicately blow her nose. "Actually, I went off duty at ten, but I've been hanging around to make sure he'd pull through." Dabbing at her eyes, she grimaced, embarrassed. "I know this is terribly unprofessional of me. But—well, Ross and I went together for a couple of years." Her lips trembled and she paused to get herself under control. After a moment she smiled weakly, assuring them, "He'll outlive us all—if he uses a little intelligence about his life-style, that is."

Val sagged back onto the sofa. "Thank God."

The doctor joined her there, slumping forward, her fingers massaging her temples. "I hope you don't mind. I'm beat. Twelve-hour shift, and then this. Seeing Ross again was just—" She sighed a trembling, forlorn sigh. "I couldn't stand it if he'd—well—died."

Val exchanged glances with Quaid, who recognized the matchmaking glint in her eyes. Draping her arm about the older woman's shoulders, she bent forward to say, "I tell you what, Doctor…"

The woman closed her eyes, looking haggard. "Please, call me Sondra."

"Okay, Sondra. When Ross gets out of here, why don't you and he come over to my place for dinner. I'd love to get to know you better." As an afterthought, she asked, "You aren't married are you?"

Sondra shook her head. "Divorced."

Quaid smiled inwardly. Folding his arms across his chest, he left Val to do her thing. After all, Ross had been alone for a long time. This attractive brunette doctor with soft gray eyes and a lingering affection would no doubt speed Ross's recovery markedly, with or without medical science.

His lips quirked. If Val got her way, and Quaid had little doubt that she would, there were going to be two weddings in Valdez very soon.

"Wouldn't it, Quaid?" he heard Val ask.

He turned toward the women. "Yes, dear?"

His question held an amused, teasing quality, as though he knew exactly what she was going to say. Val made a face at him behind Sondra's back. "I said, wouldn't it be fun for Sondra and Ross to have dinner with us?"

"I'll bring the wine," Sondra chimed in, appearing much revived.

"I'd make that dried salmon if I were you," he suggested, grinning at Sondra's sudden, perplexed expression.

Val laughed, patting the doctor's shoulder. "That reminds me, we'd better go—now that we know Ross is out of danger." Rising, she took Quaid's proffered hand, adding, "I've got a couple of hungry animals to feed back at my place." She felt Quaid run his thumb seductively along the inside of her wrist, and a delightful, familiar ache began to blossom deep within her.

When Sondra rose, Quaid said, "Tell Ross we'll be by in the morning. And tell him to shape up."

"Oh, I can promise you I will," Sondra vowed, her voice edged with the determination of a woman who has long-term plans for a man. "But, why don't you give him until, say, late afternoon before visiting." Smiling, she added, "Don't worry about him. I'm off duty tomorrow, but I plan to stay with him for as long as it takes."

"As long as it takes," Quaid echoed, draping a possessive arm about Val's shoulders. Shifting his gaze to the deceptively fragile profile of the woman he loved, he murmured, "I know how she feels."

VAL ADDED TWO PIECES of wheat toast to Quaid's breakfast tray and poured steamy coffee into a mug. Feeling light-headed from nervousness, she headed toward her room, where she'd left him sleeping soundly hours ago. It was nearly noon, and he'd fallen exhausted into bed sometime after two o'clock when they'd returned home from the hospital.

Ten minutes ago, she'd heard the shower running, so she knew he was probably famished—but, the woman in her hoped not. Juggling the tray, she knocked on her bedroom door only to have it flung open by a very virile man with shower-wet hair, his taut, muscular torso draped with a low-slung towel. "Hi, there," he said, his grin wide. Scanning the tray, he quipped, "I may be tired, Val, but I'm not bedridden."

She fought back her trepidation, masking it behind a haughty smirk. "Get back in that bed, Mr. Perrault. You need your rest today."

Elbowing him unceremoniously aside, she preceded him into the room. "I don't fix breakfast in bed for just anybody, you know." Setting the tray on the bedside table, she turned back in his direction and gave him a very direct, almost fearful look. He frowned, and she knew he'd seen her fear. Before he could react, she proceeded to drop her robe to the floor, displaying her trim torso seductively shadowed by the red mist of a lacy teddy. "And I don't *dress* like this for just anybody, either," she announced, her body thrumming with worry about how he might react.

His brows rose in surprise. "Where did you get that?" he asked, ambling over to face her, his towering presence sending a thrill of apprehension up her spine.

"Mail order from Anchorage. It came yesterday. Do you like it?" The words had come out hurriedly. Holding her breath now, she slid into the bed as nonchalantly as she could. One slender strap slipped off her shoulder, allowing the near-transparent bodice to fall low, only to be caught by one pouting nipple. It bothered her that the strap had fallen off her shoulder, but somehow, under his dark, intense scrutiny, she couldn't move to replace it.

Quaid swallowed, unaccountably touched as he

looked down at her. Valentine Larrabee, the sprightly, courageous helicopter pilot who'd long ago cast off all feminine wiles, determined to avoid erotic entanglements, was purposely transformed into a charming, if somewhat self-conscious, femme fatale.

Feeling oddly weak in his knees but extremely potent in another area of his anatomy, Quaid joined her on the bed. One hand went on its own to the lace that barely shielded her breasts, and a gentle finger traced the rise of milky flesh. "And I thought your long socks turned me on," he murmured, the sweet pain of longing registering on his face.

Her stiff little smile grew tremulous with relief, and she relaxed back into the pillows, relishing his touch and the husky resonance in his words. His dark gaze softened with tender desire, and she reached out to him. "That, my Viking, was exactly the right thing to say."

She brushed his lips lightly, adding, "It's nice to know that your becoming a celebrity hasn't made you forget your manners."

He pulled slightly away, his glance perplexed. "What are you talking about?"

Laughter gurgled in her throat as she pressed him down to the bed and snuggled in the crook of his arm. "Have you forgotten? You conquered Death Scream yesterday."

He frowned, as though the thought hadn't occurred to him. "It's funny. I have no memory of finishing it," he admitted, his voice low and melancholy. "I was too damned scared, I suppose."

She turned in his arms to be able to better view his troubled face. "It's human to be afraid, darling." Running her fingers through his damp hair, she whispered, "But you fought your fear and beat it."

When he didn't speak, only looked into her eyes, his

expression thoughtful, she decided he was ready to hear the rest, telling him carefully, "I've had some calls this morning. The *Valdez Vanguard* wants an interview." His gaze grew alert, disturbed, but she hurried on, "KVAK and KCHU are clamoring for an on-air play-by-play. Even CBS news has been on the line. Apparently an amateur photographer got some spectacular telephoto shots of you free-soloing up there and sold them to the network."

With a groan, Quaid lay back to stare at the ceiling. "Hell. What did you tell them?"

She dipped her fingers into the band of his towel, and slowly, erotically pulled it open. As the terry fabric fell away to reveal his splendid nudity, she slid up to nip his collarbone and assured him, "I told them you were too physically drained to be interviewed today."

He shifted his gaze to meet the knowing twinkle in her blue eyes—eyes he had grown to love, eyes the color of sturdy ice. His lips twisted in a crooked grin. "Too physically drained, am I?"

She nodded, sliding up to drape his massive chest with her thinly clad breasts. "Uh-huh. That's true, isn't it?"

"Oh, absolutely." His rich chuckle tickled her flesh. "I'm a physically drained man." Giving lie to that statement, he shifted her lacy torso so that she could feel the swell of his passion at the sensitive apex of her legs. She sighed languidly, knowing they would have at least this afternoon alone before Quaid would be besieged by the world outside.

As he slowly, deftly removed the scrap of lace from her body, she dropped her head back onto the pillows, enjoying his intimate assistance. When she was naked beneath him and he was threading his long fingers through her hair, an errant question came to her, and despite the inappropriateness of the time and place, she had to ask, "What do you plan to name Death Scream now that you've beaten it?"

Levering his body forward, he covered her nakedness with his own gloriously nude physique. "You have a beautiful body," he uttered, his voice harsh with desire. Slanting his lips across hers, he traced her mouth with his tongue.

She smiled inwardly. Apparently he hadn't heard her question. Teasing him, she murmured against his lips, "Well—it's a little long, but..."

"Long?" He paused in his dizzying quest with his tongue, lifting his head a scant inch away. "You've never complained before."

When Val met his twinkling gaze, she realized that he too was kidding her, and their laughter mingled in their utter, unbounded happiness to be alive and alone and in love with each other.

When the laughter died away and their gazes once again reflected their unquenched passions, Quaid kissed her deeply, thoroughly and with such a slow, tantalizing completeness that she was lifted away to divine heights. Floating above the chaste, frozen earth where they dwelt, Val and Quaid found a white-hot land, where colors came in bright bursts and souls blended in joyous, frenzied oblivion.

And while they drifted there, riding the tide of heady emotion, Val gave Quaid her heart, her soul and pledged herself to him forever. By helping him in his battle for courage, she had learned that love transcends the myths of storybook heroes. Quaid had proved to be no god, no knight in shining armor, but a mere mortal with flaws, foibles and fears. Nothing more or less than a man.

With her love, her strength, he had met and beaten his personal devil. Ironically, with his victory, by some miracle, her own devils disappeared. She felt clean, renewed and whole—because of Quaid's love, his strength. Love, it seemed, was a never-ending, ever-renewing process. A simple yet enduring truth, and Val clung to it as Quaid's lovemaking brought her exquisite release.

Joined together, their passions, for the moment, spent, Val lay atop her gentle Viking and whispered shyly, "I have a secret, Quaid."

"Tell me, sweetheart," he murmured, running mesmerizing fingers through her hair.

"You didn't have to climb Death Scream to prove to me that you're the hardest of the hard men."

Their eyes came together tenderly. With a low growl of renewed desire, he wrapped her in his arms. With a lazy smile, he murmured, "Now, that, my little village virgin, was exactly the right thing to say."

With a tormenting thrust of his hips, Quaid drew from her a tremulous cry. And once again, desire surging quick and hot through their entwined bodies, they hastened away to a secret place of pagan delights—a place the Vikings call Valhalla.

_____ Epilogue _____

THE FRETFUL GURGLE of a baby caught Val's attention, and she turned away from stirring the gravy for Christmas dinner. Quaid stood framed in the kitchen doorway, looking quaintly bemused, holding a fussy baby in the crook of one arm while he tried to slip a blue bootie onto a stubborn, flailing little foot.

She smiled, crossing her arms before her. "Having a little trouble, Daddy?"

He lifted his gaze, his expression opening in a wry grin. "Your son hates clothes."

"Oh? When he's being obstinate he's *my* son?" She laughed. "For your information, he takes after his father when it comes to throwing off his clothes."

Finally getting the bootie on, Quaid lifted the baby to his shoulder and began patting the squirming infant to ease his cranky babble. "I beg your pardon," he countered, ambling toward her in that lazy, sexy way he had. "Just so we get this understood. It's your fault I spend so much time naked." Tipping her chin up with a gentle finger, he kissed her. The baby was whimpering now and rooting around his father's shoulder. Quaid glanced at his son, at the small head covered with feathery black hair. "Think he's hungry?"

Val checked the kitchen clock. "I fed him thirty minutes ago. Probably sleepy." Holding out her arms, she said, "If you can stir the gravy, I'll put him to bed. Answer the door when Ross and Sondra get here, okay?"

"I'd rather you put me to bed, too."

Adjusting her son's blanket so that it didn't obscure his angelic face, she admonished softly, "You're insatiable, Quaid Perrault. How I put up with it, I'll never know."

The grin he flashed her was wicked and knowing as he took her into his arms, baby and all. He kissed her soundly, thoroughly, rekindling the welcome reasons why she put up with a man whose sexual appetites were so wide and varied that he could always turn her into giddy mush.

A knock on the door drew a frustrated groan from Quaid. Val hurried off, a giggle rising in her throat, as Quaid strode to the door, closely followed by a yelping Billy Bob.

"Merry Christmas," chimed Ross as he tossed a handful of squaw candy across the room, diverting Billy Bob's attention from him, his arm load of packages and his very pregnant wife, Dr. Sondra Knox. "So, where's Nathan Ross, my godson? With you two living at Gumford, I haven't even gotten to lay my eyes on him. Now that's a crime!"

Quaid took Sondra's coat. "You'll see him after his nap when he's fresh. He has an attitude when he's tired."

Ross laughed, depositing the stack of presents under the spreading spruce that stood near the door. Shrugging off his wool jacket, he kidded, "Sounds like his old man."

Sondra took Ross's arm as he helped her to the couch, remarking brightly, "You should talk. You're a regular bear when you're worn-out."

"Me?" he asked with mock incredulity as he helped her to her seat.

Ross asked Quaid, "Say, how's Val's work going down there at Gumford? Is she flying any incorrigible bears out into the wilderness?"

Quaid smiled. "Every so often. Most of the time she transports scientists and visitors to and from the reserve."

"I can't imagine her piloting a helicopter with a crazed bear in the back seat," Sondra remarked.

"It's not quite that way. The bear is caged and tranquilized, and I'm always along with my Winchester— just in case."

"It certainly smells delicious in here," Sondra said. "Val is such a wonderful cook." She leaned back and sighed, tiredly, "I'm a lousy cook, myself."

Ross sat down beside her, draping her shoulders with a sheltering arm. "You don't have to be a good cook, honey. You're a great doctor. Besides, I love to cook."

Val came out of the bedroom, closing the door silently behind her. "In that case, Ross, you can give me a hand in the kitchen." She walked over to Sondra and hugged her shoulders. "How are the twins?"

The older woman patted her belly. "They sleep all day and run marathons all night, but all the tests say they're fine, healthy girls."

Val took Ross's hand, leading him toward the kitchen. Though Quaid would rather have been the one helping his wife in the kitchen, he took a seat next to Sondra to keep her company.

Turning to better face him, Sondra touched his hand and murmured, "Did I ever thank you?" Cocking her head toward the kitchen, she added, "For saving him?" When Quaid merely looked at her, surprise at her unexpected remark reflecting in his gaze, she patted his hand. "And thanks for giving him the privilege of naming Death Scream."

Quaid looked down at her hand on his. "I never heard—what is it called now?"

"Slice of Hell."

A faint smile lifted his lips. "Fits." After a brief pause when they could hear Ross and Val laughing over something in the kitchen, Quaid asked, "Is he climbing anymore?"

"No. He's finally quit denying his heart condition. I know he misses it, but come February, he'll have his hands full with the girls. What about you? Do you miss it?"

With an almost negligible shake of his head, he said, "Considering everything—no. With Val, Nathan and my brownies, I've got other priorities now."

"I understand—and I'm happy for you."

Quaid met her pretty gray eyes again, but he said nothing.

After an awkward gap of time, she said, "We're glad you came back to Valdez for Christmas. We've been dying to see the baby ever since you wrote that he'd been born five weeks ago."

"We'll always plan to spend Christmas here in this cabin."

"Ross tells me you have a glorious retreat in Switzerland and a lovely place in Hawaii." She shifted to find a more comfortable position. "I'd think you would rather be in the islands at this time of year."

Val came to the kitchen door, wiping her hands on a towel. "We want Nathan to spend Christmas among our close friends, here, where Quaid and I met."

Sondra smiled up at her. "That's sweet."

"What's sweet?" Ross asked, coming to stand beside Val, carrying a steaming green bean casserole between two mitt-swathed hands.

"You are, darling," Sondra told him with an impish smile. "And you look as cute as a button in that pink apron."

"Don't I know it." Ross beamed at her. "Not just any

man could make such a frilly fashion statement and re-
tain his raging masculinity."

Amid easy laughter, Val announced that dinner was
ready. Quaid helped Sondra from the sagging couch,
and they all converged on the kitchen table, overflow-
ing with delectable fare.

As Quaid helped Val into her chair, he brushed her
ear with a kiss, whispering, "I have a present for you."

She raised a loving gaze to his face and their eyes
met softly. "Me, too."

A well-shaped brow rose. Though his expression remained mild, his gaze twinkled with wicked promise.
"Bedtime?"

"How did you guess?"

His only response was a rich, explicit chuckle.
Squeezing her shoulders, he drew his hands reluctantly away.

"What the hell were you two whispering about?"
Ross queried, his expression suspicious.

"Shut up, silly man," Sondra admonished. "Pass the
dressing."

"Oh, *that*..." Ross grinned sheepishly at Quaid.
"We'll eat fast."

Surrounded by relaxed conversation, Quaid and Val
enjoyed a close-knit holiday feast with friends. And
later, they exchanged their gifts as promised—gifts
that had nothing to do with their affluence. In complete
harmony with the season, they gave to each other a re-
newal of their wedding vows—to lend to each other
their strengths, accept their weaknesses and, in a joyous leap of faith, entrust each other with their unfailing
devotion.

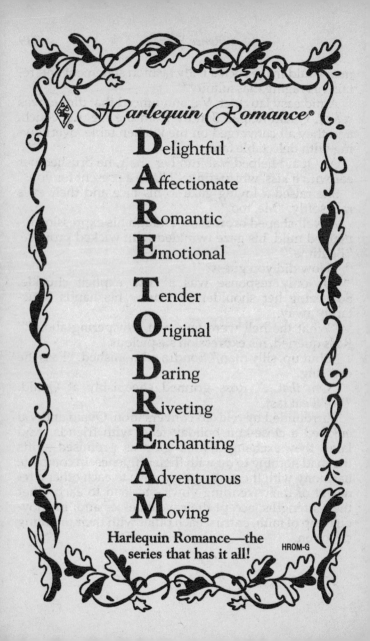

Harlequin Romance®

Delightful

Affectionate

Romantic

Emotional

Tender

Original

Daring

Riveting

Enchanting

Adventurous

Moving

Harlequin Romance—the
series that has it all!

HROM-G

HARLEQUIN  PRESENTS®

HARLEQUIN PRESENTS
men you won't be able to resist
falling in love with…

HARLEQUIN PRESENTS
women who have feelings
just like your own…

HARLEQUIN PRESENTS
powerful passion in
exotic international settings…

HARLEQUIN PRESENTS
intense, dramatic stories that will keep you
turning to the very last page…

HARLEQUIN PRESENTS
The world's bestselling romance series!

Harlequin® Historical

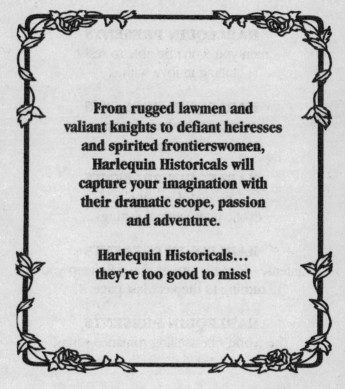

From rugged lawmen and
valiant knights to defiant heiresses
and spirited frontierswomen,
Harlequin Historicals will
capture your imagination with
their dramatic scope, passion
and adventure.

Harlequin Historicals...
they're too good to miss!

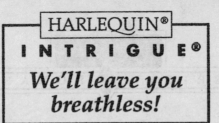

LOOK FOR OUR FOUR FABULOUS MEN!

Each month some of today's bestselling authors bring four new fabulous men to Harlequin American Romance. Whether they're rebel ranchers, millionaire power brokers or sexy single dads, they're all gallant princes—and they're all ready to sweep you into lighthearted fantasies and contemporary fairy tales where anything is possible and where all your dreams come true!

You don't even have to make a wish…
Harlequin American Romance will grant your every desire!

Look for Harlequin American Romance
wherever Harlequin books are sold!